WHILE YOU WERE SPELLBOUND

CHRISTINE ZANE THOMAS

1

CURSES AND CAR ALARMS

Not for the first time, I was in my own head. Entranced by thoughts of what could've been, what should've been, and fearful of what was to come. Things had gotten crazy over the past two years, and it didn't seem like they were slowing down anytime soon.

At least tonight, this head game was my own doing. I wasn't put there by a spell or because a demon found their way inside my mind. Both had happened before. Neither were pleasant experiences.

This wasn't either.

It was me getting in my own way—blocking out the rest of the world as I got hung up on so many things outside of my control.

I'd gone the last few blocks on autopilot, barely registering the curses being thrown in my direction. These weren't the witchy kind of curses, though they were uttered by the lips of a witch.

My best friend, Trish Harris, was nearly a block behind me now. I'd zoned out and set my own pace. Trish couldn't match me stride for stride. She was at least a foot shorter than me. As always, she wore her blocky Doc Martins, while I had comfortable sneakers. In her all-black attire, Trish blended into the night.

The witching hour was upon us. It was just after midnight and Embassy Row was dark and *mostly* quiet— aside from her curses.

Regardless of what I wore—which was dark jeans and a navy hoodie—I was going to stand out. My blonde hair reflected every streetlight.

Even the full moon gave me away when it peeked out from behind the clouds.

Somewhere in the mountains, a werewolf was hiding the night away. He was in the forefront of my thoughts.

I stopped in the middle of the sidewalk, just ahead of the next crosswalk, and allowed Trish to catch up.

Behind us, down Massachusetts Avenue, Dupont Circle was still bustling with tourists and local night life. Up the hill ahead toward the Naval Observatory, the sidewalk was empty.

The houses were all dark, aside from the occasional lamp. Every house for the next quarter of a mile had a flag on display. Some had flagpoles right outside their front steps. Others had staffs angled from balconies and walls, proudly displaying their country's colors.

We'd passed Kenya, Haiti, and Korea, plus a host of other flags I didn't recognize. The flags of Japan and Turkey fluttered against a gust of wind.

I'd already returned to my restless mind when a shrieking car alarm roused me from my stupor.

A familiar chill ran up my spine. Something I hadn't felt in a while—a hint of danger in the air.

I slowed to a stop with the hairs on my neck prickling and magic flowed to my fingertips. I was ready for a fight.

Ready to fight—to wield magic for the first time in months.

That's how long it'd been since I'd needed to use my powers.

Magic only works when someone needs it most. When in mortal peril. When in dire straits. Or sometimes—at least in my experience—when you've left the clean towels in the dryer and already gotten into the shower.

The magic hummed with its own frequency, the warmth flowing from my chest to my fingers. It felt like home.

The past few months had been a blur—ever since my mother had come back from the near dead. For decades, her soul had been interred in a vessel—an enclosure of mortal substance. In other words, she'd been trapped in the body of an owl. Her original mortal vessel—my mother's body— was stolen.

That wasn't even the worst of it. For the past couple of years, the thief—a familiar named Morgana—had made my life hell. Literally. She'd sent demons after me, one of which had killed my father. Then she'd enlisted the help of a hunter—a mortal who hunts down paranormals like me and my shifter friends.

It was all for naught. I'd won. I'd beat her. Sort of. Morgana had gotten away, but not without surrendering my mother's body.

The last few months had been quiet. Or quiet by my standards.

No Morgana. She seemed to have disappeared without a trace. Literally. Brad hadn't been able to trace her through the Shadow Realm. Nor had I been able to summon her using other magical means.

At least there'd been no murders. And no magical beings escaping the shadow realm to rampage on earth.

Even the Faction—the underground society of witches and wizards I belonged to—didn't have a lot going on.

Not until tonight.

I'd spent the past few months nursing my mother back to health.

We had a daily routine. Once she got out of bed, we went for a walk. We drank copious amounts of coffee. Watched TV. Ate dinner. Watched more TV. Ate a midnight snack. Then I'd go to bed while she stayed up and watched even more TV. We'd do the same thing again the next day.

It was like living with Gran, only a lot quieter. Not only was my mother's circadian rhythm off, she had other issues as well. She could barely string three words together. Turns out being mostly an owl for a couple of decades isn't good for you.

Thanks to our routine, she was getting stronger and more lucid. Also, thanks to our routine, I was feeling the opposite. It was probably why I was in my head so much. And why I'd jumped at the chance to get away for a weekend, taking my first official mission for the Faction.

Hence why I was on edge.

I waited for something to happen—for a mugger or a more sinister being to jump out of the shadows. Nothing. No movement at all.

The car alarm continued until finally, its lights blinked in unison with the sound of a locking mechanism.

For now, the danger was nonexistent.

Somehow, that only made things worse, and those dreadful thoughts plaguing me for the last few blocks came tumbling out my lips, "Dave's going to break up with me. I just know it."

"WHAT WAS THAT?" Trish cupped her hand behind her ear.

I looked both ways. The street was empty. Then I stepped out into the crosswalk. "I said Dave's going to break up with me.

It sounded even more wrong the second time. And right. I wasn't a psychic but the signs were there.

"That's what I thought you said." Trish followed me out into the street. "Mind telling me why you're harboring such a crazy idea?"

"Just a feeling."

"A feeling—like those feelings you've had before?"

I shook my head. "I don't seem to have those powers anymore. Not since—"

Trish nodded. "Not since your Gran left. Same here."

We'd both been given gifts—special abilities from Mother Gaia. We both seemed to have lost them when Gran crossed over to the *other* side with Mother Gaia.

"I bet Gran had something to do with her taking them away."

"I'm not a betting person," Trish said. "But I'd put money on that one. So, why's Dave going to break up with you?"

"The normal reasons," I said. "We've drifted apart. I barely see him. I don't even sleep over at his house anymore. I practically moved out to take care of Mom."

She huffed and stopped in the crosswalk. I could practically hear her eyes roll. "Dave Marsters is not breaking up with you. He'd be out of his mind to do that."

"No," I scoffed. "He'd be sensible—which he totally is. He's out of his mind to try and keep things the way they are —with me and Mom and everything that's happened since I moved to Creel Creek."

"None of which you caused," she said.

"But all of which I'm responsible for."

Trish just gave me one of her looks.

Disregarding the short-statured witch, a red and gray taxi inched toward the stop sign behind her, its headlights beaming into our faces.

Trish leveled her already cold gaze at the taxi, and it stopped inching. "You can't shoulder all the blame. So what, some shit went down and you were there. It doesn't make any of it *your* fault."

"Should I blame my mom?" I asked her. "She can barely speak."

"Blame Morgana," Trish said.

"I've tried." I really had.

Except every time I thought about Morgana, it brought many other mixed feelings to the surface. I still had questions—questions I didn't think I could get the answers to. Not with Mom in the state she was in.

And not without Morgana.

Questions like how had my mother gotten wrapped up in all this? Why had she joined the Faction in the first place? And what was she supposed to be doing when Morgana sprung her trap?

None of it mattered now. I just wanted Trish to move out of the crosswalk and out of the taxi's way, but she was rooted to the spot. "Okay. So, what are you going to do about it?"

"About what?"

"About Dave."

"Oh." I shrugged. "I haven't really thought that far ahead. I guess I should just move somewhere. Me and Mom. Get out of yours—Dave's—everyone's hair."

Trish glared at me.

The cab moved forward a few feet, trying to edge around her. Its bumper was close, not touching, but close to Trish's rear end.

It wasn't a smart move. Neither was the honk—just a light tap on the horn to let her know he was annoyed.

The problem was, she got annoyed too.

A curse—a real one—flew from her lips. Her fingers moved in an arc above the hood. The engine sputtered and died.

"He was just trying to do his job," I defended him.

"Yeah, well, I'm just trying to be your friend right now. It's just as hard." She twirled her finger again and the taxi's engine came back to life. She kicked the rear bumper with a Doc Martin and said, "Go on. Get out of here."

With a screech of its tires, it took off up Massachusetts Avenue like a bat out of hell.

"Where were we?" she asked. "Oh, that's right. You were being an idiot."

"Me? An idiot? Look who's still in the street."

She sighed and finally began walking again, trudging up the sidewalk behind me. "You know what I mean," she said. "You can't leave us now. You're a part of Creel Creek. Just as much as me or anyone else. Plus, Dave needs you. You make him better. He makes you better."

"You really don't think he'd be better off without me?"

"I don't," she said. "He loves you. You love him. And that's all that's going to matter in the end."

"What end?" I asked her.

"I don't know." She shrugged. "Some end. Endings are inevitable."

2

WHAT WE DISCUSS IN THE SHADOWS

For the next block, Trish abandoned her curses and complaints. She kept telling me how silly I was to think Dave would want to break up, and she kept feeding me reasons I couldn't move away.

I was just happy she was keeping up.

"Let's not forget," she went on, "you're a vital part of Bewitched Books."

"I am not!" I snorted. "If you came in three hours earlier, you wouldn't even need me."

She stopped again, breathing heavy. "Like I said, you're vital. Those are three critical hours of sleep. My smartwatch says I need them. And it says I've reached my step goal. How much farther? I swear it didn't take this long in daylight."

"That's cause we took an Uber."

"Remind me again, why we couldn't just do that tonight?"

"Element of surprise?" I shrugged. I didn't have a good reason.

I'd wanted a little more time to think. I'd accepted this

mission on a whim, and I hadn't planned out anything except getting here.

"I thought you said this was a diplomatic mission." If it wasn't so dark, I would've seen one of Trish's perfectly groomed eyebrows raise a notch above the other.

"It is," I said.

"Then why do you need the element of surprise?"

"We, uh, don't. And technically, I never said *our* mission was diplomatic."

"But you did."

"I can see how it might've come across that way. It's their mission that's diplomatic. Hence the embassies."

"Constance! Remind me why—"

"Wait. That reminds me." A figurative lightbulb went on above my head. I'd almost forgotten something I'd sworn not to forget. This whole over forty thing was filled with minefields. Like going into a room and forgetting what I went in there for.

Only forgetting this tiny thing could've been disastrous.

I pulled two sticks of gum out of my pocket. I held one out to Trish.

"Let me guess. This is for the mission." Her tone was snarky, but no more than usual.

"If I say it is, does that mean you won't take it?"

"It's your mission," she said. "I told you, I'm not part of the Faction. I'm here because I haven't been to DC in ages. I wanted to go to the museums and the zoo—which we still haven't done, by the way. You promised."

Trish had always resisted the Faction.

"I know. I know." I sighed, as exasperated with her as she was with me. "You want to see the pandas."

"More importantly, the red pandas. The others just laze around all day like your Gran used to do."

"Right. We'll see both... in the morning. Tonight, I've got to do this. Chewing the gum is a part of it. If you didn't want to participate, you could've stayed at the hotel."

I was secretly thankful she hadn't stayed at the hotel.

Trish yanked the gum from my fingers and began to unwrap the foil. "Dave would kill me if I let you walk these streets alone." She stopped before putting the innocent-looking pink stick in her mouth. "What kind of gum is this again?"

"I think it's laced with a potion," I said. "Ivan said Kalene probably forgot to use it. Hence why we're here to find her."

Trish grimaced. "Does that mean it's going to taste like a potion?"

I hadn't considered that. Like medicine, I associated potions more with their outcomes than anything else. And like most medicines, there was usually a flavor—a bad one.

"There's only one way to find out." I popped the gum in my mouth and chewed.

Taking a potion was unpleasant. Uncomfortable even. It was like swallowing the elements one after the other.

Earth—the grit of dirt between my teeth.

Wind—like my lungs might explode.

Fire—a burning sensation at the back of my throat.

And finally, water—like drinking from a fire hose.

The effects didn't last long—about the same amount of time it takes to pull the flavor from a stick of Juicy Fruit. But some lingered. I'd catch my breath only to lose it again. And there was a constant tickle in the back of my throat.

"This is weird." Trish chewed. "Lauren made this?"

I nodded.

Lauren Whittaker was a member of the Faction. She held one of the four books, the book of potions, which together made up the Faction's grimoire.

I held the book of secrets. Kalene had the book of spells. And Ivan Rush, our quasi-leader, had the register—what amounted to the Faction's family tree.

The gum was Lauren's own invention because the potion inside it had a short life, up to fifteen minutes. We didn't know how long I'd need its effects. So, Lauren came up with this solution. The gum would last for several hours.

I only hoped it was long enough—I'd given Trish my backup piece.

The truth was, I didn't know what we were heading into. Maybe a trap. Maybe nothing.

We walked another block until we reached the address I had gotten from Ivan.

"This is it?" I said the words but I wasn't convinced.

The address matched, only the exterior of the house didn't match the memory I had of it from earlier in the day.

It was a stone building, gothic in style. In daylight, I would've sworn it was made of red brick. The house was inside a fortress. Tall stone walls covered in ivy surrounded the structure, with an iron gate for access. Through it, a courtyard garden was visible. Like the other embassies, there was a flag on display. The colors were right, but their arrangement was off.

Trish read the name of the country engraved on a sign outside the gate. It sounded strange. It wasn't Transylvania, but it was close.

My memory of the word faded, so I read it out loud myself. That memory faded too. And when I looked at the sign again, it was like reading it for the first time. "That's trippy."

"It's more than trippy," Trish said. "That's some powerful magic. A witch did this. No way a vampire could pull off a memory charm this powerful."

All supernatural beings are inherently magic. Shifters use the magic to change form. Vampires use theirs to lure victims—read minds and the like.

There are even Fae walking among us with dormant magical energy hidden deep in their DNA. They can't call it up and wield it like we do, but it's there all the same.

I'd seen something like this before in the League of Artemis, a fraternal organization of shifters. There was a room imbued with magic, put there by its makers. Its walls could tell stories. And inside it, no one could tell a lie.

I was the first witch to ever set foot in that room.

"It used to be easier to call upon magic," I said. "I'm not saying you're wrong, but there's a chance a vampire did do this. Think about how long they live. There's got to be a few around who know how to harness their magic and use it."

"Fair point," Trish said. "So, can I point out the obvious?"

I inclined my head.

"Doing this at night was *not* a good idea. Coming back tomorrow, in daylight, seems like the obvious choice."

"That's what they want you to think," I said. "You know vampires aren't nocturnal. Remember what killed Mr. Caulfield wasn't actually daylight—we saw him in the sunlight a hundred times—it was a potion that poisoned him."

"Yeah, but breaking in at night is equally cliché."

"We aren't breaking in," I said.

"What are you going to do, ring the doorbell?"

She made a good point. I tried the gate. It was locked.

"Guess we'll have to come back tomorrow," Trish said. "After the zoo."

Behind us, a deep male voice asked, "Are you going to see the pandas?"

3

THE VAMPIRIC EMBASSY

"Who are you?" I asked the shadowy figure behind us. My creep radar was on high alert, but I could tell immediately this was no ordinary creep of the beltway.

This was a vampire. He was tall—too tall. He had long slick hair and big dark eyes that never seemed to blink.

Instinctively, I cowered closer to the iron gate only to realize that my instincts were all wrong. I'd essentially trapped myself.

Lucky for me, Trish never cowers. She pointed her trigger finger at him, a spell at the ready. Magic hummed in the air.

"You must be Constance Campbell," he said to me. "I was expecting you today, albeit a little earlier."

"Yeah, well, we were busy," I lied.

"*Not* seeing the pandas." Trish scoured the street behind.

I assumed she was wondering the same thing I was— where exactly had he come from? And how did he sneak up on us like that?

There was an obvious answer.

Vampire.

Against my better judgment, I asked him, "Where were you just now?"

"Just out for a bite." He smiled—actually smiled—revealing larger than average incisors. They were both lengthy and sharp. There was a sheen of something dark, maybe crimson, on all of his teeth.

"Oh, right." Ask stupid questions, get spine-chilling answers.

"It's a pleasure to finally meet you, Miss Campbell. My name is Carlos Ortega. And this is my house you're attempting to break into."

"We weren't breaking in," Trish argued. "In fact, we were just about to leave."

I said, "We were going to knock on the door first."

"You were going to knock on the door?" Carlos was not convinced. "At midnight?"

Trish flipped her hair out of her face, her scowl clear in the moonlight. "You *are* vampires, are you not?"

"We are vampires," he agreed. "But you Faction witches aren't stupid. You know full well we don't sleep in coffins all day."

"A—I'm not with the faction. She is." Trish waggled her *loaded* finger in his direction. In many circles, the gesture would've been seen as a threat. "And B—I know vampires don't sleep at all. So what does it matter what time of day we come calling at your door?"

Carlos was unfazed. "Fair enough. Let me unlock the gate and invite you inside. Oh! That's right. You don't *have* to be invited, now, do you?"

"Hardy har." Trish shook her head.

"Wait," I whispered to her, "is that a real thing or another myth?"

"It's a thing," Trish said. "Let's just get on with this. I hate formalities. It's half the reason I'm not in the Faction."

"May I ask about the other half?" Carlos twisted an ancient key in the metal lock and the iron gate creaked open. He swung it wide and ushered us through the garden to the house.

"It's nothing personal," Trish said. "I just have a thing about other people. I tend not to like them."

"That sounds altogether personal," Carlos quipped. He produced another, smaller key and opened the door of the house.

In stark contrast to the shadowy inner garden, the light from the foyer was blinding. A chandelier hung from the high ceiling, its crystals sparkling with reflected light.

There was a sitting room to the left. Every piece of furniture was pristine. A double stairway wrapped the walls, hiding the first floor from view and leading to an unseen second floor.

Trish gaped at the ornate beauty. "What is this place?"

"It's the Vampiric Embassy," I said.

"But like, what do you do here?" she asked Carlos.

"It's a sanctuary of sorts. We offer our protection to vampires seeking refuge."

"What type of protection?"

"Legal and *other* forms," he said. "Vampires, as I'm sure you're aware, are often made out to be villains. Go figure. A couple of bad years and one dreadful book made for generations of prejudice."

"Movies too," Trish added. "You still haven't answered the question. What exactly do you do here?"

"We liaise, often with the government—from Congress to local municipalities. Other times, with organizations like the Faction. Especially if they're out to blame vampires for crimes they didn't commit. I've seen vampires run out of communities after decades of living peacefully because of minor misunderstandings. In cases like that, we help them get a fresh start."

"And this is your home?" Trish asked.

"I could give you the tour." The vampire's dark eyes went to the second floor. "Or we could get down to business."

"Business." I thought surely Trish would say the same.

To my surprise, she said, "Tour."

Carlos raised an eyebrow. "Which is it?"

They both looked at me. "The tour is fine, I guess. As long as it starts with Kalene. Where is she?"

"Kalene?" He gave away nothing. "The witch I met last week? Is she lost?"

"She was here, under *your* protection," I said, exactly as Ivan had described it to me.

He shook his head sadly. "I'm sorry, but she lost that protection almost as soon as it was granted. I don't extend it to spies. Not in my own home."

Carlos was more cognizant of the details than I was. I only knew what Ivan wanted me to know, which apparently wasn't much.

Had she really been spying?

I'd been so primed to take the mission, I'd failed to question it.

Now, I had a lot of questions. Why *had* Kalene gone to the Vampiric Embassy? And if she wasn't here, then where could she be?

Anywhere.

"Surely, the Faction can understand the predicament she put us in?"

"Us?"

Trish had latched onto the word too. "How many vampires live here?"

"A few," he said. "But it's just us here tonight. And it is we who are in the predicament. I can't allow a spy to leave the premises—not without knowing what she knows. Or without something from you in return."

"So she *is* here?"

"She's here," Carlos relented. "I can assure you she's come to no harm."

"Your assurances don't mean a lot," I said. "I don't exactly know you. Plus, the whole vampire thing."

"Books and movies," he sighed.

"I want to see Kalene."

"Fine." He smiled and this time it wasn't nearly as wicked as it had looked outside in the dark. "This way."

Carlos led us up the stairs and at the first landing, muttered to Trish, "I'm beginning to believe you about the Faction. They do seem to have a people problem."

Trish smirked. "And she's one of the good ones."

"Figures." At the top of the stairs, the vampire put a finger to his lips. He knocked gingerly on the first door in a long and narrow hallway. "Kalene," he said, "your friends are here."

"Friends?" Her sleepy voice barely penetrated the door.

A moment later, she opened it with a yawn and a smile. Kalene's normally braided hair was down; it was so long it grazed her backside. Over her pajamas she wore a robe embroidered with a crest—a sword and a skull wrapped in feathery wings in the colors of the flag outside.

She had been here a few days, but her room was tidy. It looked like the guest room of an older relative. There was a four-poster bed, a nightstand, a bookshelf, but no TV.

Assuming she could find something to read, I was sure it

suited Kalene fine. She didn't own a television. Her shelves at home were filled with paperbacks.

At one time, I'd thought her peculiar and a tad naive. What I'd mistaken for nosiness was gumption. No matter the circumstances, she was always serious.

The look on her face now was anything but serious. She was out of it—dazed and confused. "Carlos," she said serenely, "my friends are here. Hi, friends."

"That's what I said." He smiled genuinely. "They'd like to take you home."

"But they can't do that."

"Why not?" Trish and I asked in unison.

"Cause I was bad." Kalene's drawl was more pronounced than usual. "During the party, I snuck into *his* office. He caught me there and he won't let me go."

"I *will* let you go," Carlos retorted. "All you have to do is tell me what you were here for. What did you take?"

"I'll never tell."

Trish pinched the bridge of her nose, then turned to Carlos. "Can't you save us all a few minutes and just read her mind?"

"Afraid not," he said. "It's been spelled against being read. I can see all the thoughts that pop in her brain, save anything about her spying."

When it came to other paranormals, I found it hard to separate fact from fiction. There was just too much to learn. But I did know vampires had mind powers. They could read thoughts. Not every thought—just those at the forefront of the mind.

Except those weren't the only mind powers they had. A spell was protecting Kalene's secret, but she'd become susceptible to his mind control—another aspect of vampiric mind power that I knew little about.

I did have some protection. I chewed my gum with renewed vigor.

"Now, are you ready for the tour?"

"Sure." I shrugged.

"What about her?" Trish pointed at Kalene who still looked loopy.

"Gather your things," Carlos told Kalene. "Meet us in the sitting room in ten minutes."

The grand tour took about ten minutes. The whole upper floor was living quarters. The downstairs was more formal. There were offices, a kitchen, and a banquet hall. We circled back to the sitting room where Kalene was waiting for us, a bag in hand.

"Wait here. I'll be right back." Carlos went down the hallway toward his office.

"We could bolt," Trish said. "The door's right there. No one's stopping us."

"What if he comes back?"

Trish waggled a finger. "We go out, magic guns blazing."

"It wouldn't work," Kalene said softly. "He has me spellbound. I can't leave."

"Right." I nudged Trish. "You're still chewing the gum, right?"

She nodded.

"Chewing that gum is one thing," Carlos called from the hallway. "I may not hear *your* inner thoughts or have the ability to ensnare your mind, but I still have excellent hearing. I can't believe you'd treat me like that. And after I gave you the tour, too."

Right. Vampire.

"You know," he called. "Mr. Rush suggested an even trade. You for her."

"Me?" I cried. "I'm not going to be your prisoner."

"No. No. Nothing like that." He glided back into the room "This would be an exchange of skills. Mr. Rush tells me you're quite the problem solver. You've solved a few mysteries for the Faction and the local sheriff?"

"She has," Trish answered. "What's it to you, Count Dracula?"

The vampire threw several newspapers on an antique coffee table.

"What's this?" I asked, picking up a copy of *The Eerie Enquirer*, a paranormal tabloid. Like many others, it used to be displayed prominently in supermarkets across the country. Now, it could only be found in select cities. Creel Creek was one of them. I recognized it from the brief time I worked at the grocery store.

"This is our trade," Carlos said. "Unless *you* can tell me the secrets Kalene stole?"

"I can't," I told him. "I don't know why she came here."

Carlos sank into a leather chair. He rested his chin on a fist and studied me. "You know what? I believe you. That's why I'm making you this offer."

"What exactly are you offering?" Trish rifled the tabloids. "What's all this about?"

"Missing persons," he answered. "All of them have the same trait. They fit a pattern of sorts."

"What pattern?"

"They all had trouble sleeping."

"So do I," Trish said. "How does that have anything to do with you or the Faction? Can you get to the point? It's late. I'm ready to get back to the hotel and not sleep."

"The point is, they all claimed to have had bad dreams."

"I'm not following," I said.

"Shortly before their disappearances, they had trouble sleeping. Almost as if something was attacking their mind.

Tell me, Miss Campbell, do you know the signs a vampire is feeding on you?"

I shook my head.

"Strange dreams," Trish said. "Bite marks on your neck. Tiredness but unwilling to go to sleep."

"It's the saliva," Carlos said. "It's a stimulant, like caffeine."

"Okay. I'm starting to understand. The M.O. of these disappearances fits vampire involvement. Is that where you're going with this?"

"That's what I was thinking," Trish added.

I couldn't help but wonder if Carlos had done some research on me. Did he know how many mysteries I'd gotten caught up in? Only some of which were currently solved...

"What does this have to do with Kalene?" I asked.

"Nothing at all," Carlos said. "It's a puzzle—a puzzle I want solved."

"Why?" I asked. "Why don't you try and catch whoever's doing this yourself?"

"First and foremost, it's not my job," Carlos said. "My job is here in Washington. But the Faction—this *is* the type of thing you do, is it not?"

"He's got a point." Trish bobbed her head in my direction. "Will you go ahead and agree so we can get out of here?"

"I can't. I'm not exactly in a good place to go traipsing across the country looking for a killer."

"You won't have to." Carlos stood as if to usher us out. "Like I said, it follows a pattern. I'll let you guess what city is in the middle of said pattern."

I didn't have to say it, but I did. "Creel Creek?"

"Afraid so."

Trish huffed. "Just when we were getting comfortable, a vampire shows up."

"Ah, but you never let me finish," Carlos sounded triumphant. "The other reason this isn't a case for me? A vampire isn't committing these crimes. This last piece of evidence comes from a podcast released this morning. I believe you might've heard of it. It's called *Creel Creek After Dark*."

4

CREEL CREEK AFTER DARK

EPISODE 139

It's getting late.
Very late.
You hear something go bump in the night.
Are you afraid?
You should be!
Welcome to Creel Creek After Dark: Season Two - The Haunting
Season.

I vana: I'm your host, Ivana Steak. With me, are my cohorts and cohosts, Athena Hunter and Mister Rush.

Rush: Good evening, folks.

Athena: Hello, paranormal world. You look lovely today. Ivana, I have to say, I get goosebumps listening to the new intro.

Rush: It's the cello in the background. Gets me every time too.

Athena: That's probably it. Either way, I'm glad Ivana suggested we do something different for season two. Come to that, I'm glad you suggested a season two, Mister Rush.

What a great way to mark the changes we've been through in the past year or so.

Ivana: I just hope our listeners and those viewing on ParaTube enjoy the changes.

Athena: Which reminds me—they can subscribe to ParaTube for just six dollars a month. That subscription comes with unlimited access to shows like this one and more. And don't forget to review and shoot us a like on all the social media channels. But who am I kidding? Y'all know and you've probably already done all that!

Ivana: Don't jump to conclusions, Athena. We might have a few first-timers. If this is your first time joining us, you're in for a treat. Tonight, we're discussing a few *trivial* matters.

Athena: Obviously the word trivial is dripping with sarcasm. My only question is, are you talking the robbery at the bank this morning or how the county continues to stall on those courthouse repairs?

Ivana: Neither. We're talking about all those disappearances in the last year.

Rush: I did hear something about the robbery. Supposedly, the perp doesn't remember doing it. Or rather, he says it happened in a dream. What's your take on that?

Athena: Sounds like a terrible defense to me.

Rush: Ivana?

Ivana: I, for one, believe him.

Athena: Seriously? It sounds to me like this guy got caught with his finger in his jacket and now he wants to plead insanity.

Rush: I'm with you, Athena. But it brings up a good topic.

Ivana: And that is?

Rush: Dreams. They're sort of magic, aren't they? We get to step into worlds of our own creation. They connect to us in ways that defy our own logic. We get to talk to loved ones who've passed away. We get to star in the movie. Sometimes I wake up and believe I won that lottery or met a beautiful woman—quite literally the woman of my dreams—only to figure out a few minutes later I didn't do any of that. And my bank account balance is still way closer to zero than I'd like it to be.

Athena: That was probably his problem too.

Rush: Funny.

Ivana: I don't feel as connected to my dreams as you do, Rush.

Rush: That's a shame. It really is.

Athena: So, back to the robbery. What are you saying? Do you think he was sleepwalking?

Rush: No. I'm not saying that. I'm saying dreams are their own sort of reality. It's easy to get things mixed up. Another thing about dreams is your subconscious is in control.

Athena: He was still there, right? He wasn't in dreamland. It happened in the bank. It was all on camera.

Ivana: I think you're missing Rush's point. And we're way off today's topic. Remember? I wanted to discuss all the disappearances in the last year. Several in one night alone.

Rush: Right. Sorry to go off on a tangent like that. It won't happen again.

Athena: It's no problem, Rush. Ivana, go on. Tell us about these disappearances.

Ivana: I'll start with our local sheriff, who's done nothing. Our whole community seems to have forgotten these people. Houses are abandoned. Stores are closed. And no one seems to care. Everyone is just carrying on as if it's nothing.

Rush: If I recall, the night in question was the night of the blood moon. Correct?

Ivana: Correct.

Athena: So, who exactly is missing?

Ivana: That's the thing. I don't know. I can't remember their names either.

Athena: I'm sure many of our patrons are wondering if maybe they moved away? What do you say to that?

Ivana: And left all of their things? No. I think these folks were just the tip of the iceberg. The troubling thing is it's still happening today. Do your remember Kara Huber? We had her on the podcast last month.

Athena: The psychic who couldn't predict our futures because the energy in the room was off? Yeah. I remember her.

Ivana: Her business—which is also her house by the way—has been closed for two weeks. No one has seen her in those two weeks. I did a little digging of my own. And let's just say what I found will ensure no one turns a blind eye to these disappearances again.

THIS FOOTAGE IS courtesy of BuzzerCam Doorbells and More...

The time is 02:43:16 PM.

The sun shines brightly on the driveway of 56 North Pearl Street. At the street, there's a mailbox under a large oak tree. A sign in the front yard reads Fortunes and Palmistry. The next line says By Appointment Only.

Something disturbs the birds in the oak tree, who fan out in all directions just as an elderly woman steps out on the front porch.

Our vantage never changes.

The woman, Kara Huber, stretches. She gazes up at the commotion in the tree.

She takes the steps down to the driveway, slowly and continues to trudge down the drive.

The sun seems to rejuvenate her. She turns her face to the sky, stopping before she crosses into the shadow of the tree. Then she checks the mail.

On the way back to her porch, she's talking to herself. No one else is there. Her eyes close as she steps into the sun again.

The time is 02:45:48 PM.

There's no distortion of the picture. No blur effect, no wave, or static. The picture is crystal clear.

Kara Huber disappears.

The time is 02:45:49 PM.

Only a second has passed.

Kara Huber hasn't been seen since.

5

IN WITCH WE DRIVE

The next morning at the Smithsonian Zoo, I waged a war with guilt. I kept thinking about Dave and his girls and how I'd rather be with them on a Sunday rather than two curmudgeonly witches.

I'd missed our usual girls night when Dave is gone where we painted our toenails, ate popcorn, and I introduced them to late Eighties and early Nineties romcoms.

It wasn't like I could bring them with me. Today they were missing out on elephants, seals, and pandas, but they'd also missed out meeting a vampire. They'd spent the night in their uncle's more than capable care and got some quality time with their cousins.

I made a mental note to bring them here one day soon. And another note about Trish, who hadn't complained about the miles we'd walked so far.

Sure, she'd complained about other things, mostly having to share a bed with me while Kalene got the other. She also claimed I snored at night and that I hogged the covers.

Dave had mentioned the latter, but he'd never said

anything about the former. I swooned at the thought. It made me miss him more. And I hoped Trish was right about us.

At the zoo, she was in her happy place—if it could be called that. She was right about another thing—the red pandas were worth the price of admission. Like the other Smithsonian museums along the National Mall, the zoo was free.

After a quick lunch, we got on the road heading south for Creel Creek. The suburbs of Northern Virginia stretched for miles outside the city until the terrain changed. We left behind the beautiful homes for the much more beautiful Blue Ridge Mountains, and in the distance, Shenandoah National Park.

Kalene was sitting shotgun looking out the window. She was herself again. Mostly herself. Usually a chatterbox, she'd been quiet all morning.

I thought maybe she was embarrassed. Not only was she caught spying on the vampires, but she'd forgotten to protect herself as well.

It was a rookie mistake and Kalene was no rookie. In her short time with the Faction, she'd overcome countless other-worldly creatures. She'd done more magic than most witches do in a lifetime.

Her mother, Rainbow Moone, who I'd briefly met in the shadow realm while fighting off a demon, would've been proud of the witch she'd become.

I only wished my mother could say the same.

Trish let out a long sigh from the backseat. "So, we're really not going to talk about it?"

With her boots on one side of the car and her head on the other, Trish had sprawled out like she was a teenager in the Eighties. Granted, she once was.

"About what?" I asked her.

"About last night," she huffed.

"Oh, yeah." Kalene joined the conversation. "Thank y'all for picking me up."

"You mean bailing you out?"

I turned the radio down a notch. "We didn't bail her out," I said. "We negotiated her release."

"It wasn't much of a negotiation."

"If I recall," I glared in the rearview mirror, "you were okay with it at the time."

"Yeah, well, I was tired and grumpy."

"You're always grumpy." I shook my head. "We got Kalene back, which is what matters."

"What are you two talking about?" Kalene twisted toward the center console and eyed Trish. I checked the mirror. Trish rolled her eyes.

"What's that supposed to mean? You negotiated? You got me back?"

"It means Constance is putting her neck on the line— literally—for you. And for the Vampiric Embassy."

"I don't remember being forced to stay there against my will, if that's what you're talking about."

"That's cause it *wasn't* against your will," Trish said. "You were under Carlos's mind control."

"No, I wasn't," Kalene dismissed her. "I think I'd know if—"

"You wouldn't," Trish said. "It's kind of the point of mind control."

Kalene stuck a hand in her pocket. She yanked out a stick of gum and blinked slowly. "I... I must've forgotten. Wait—was I there last night when all this happened?"

"Sort of," Trish said.

"Sort of?"

"You ever see a video of someone who just got their wisdom teeth taken out?" Trish asked. "They're still on the anesthesia, and they're talking all funny. They'll tell you anything."

"Yeah..."

"You, last night."

Kalene slapped her forehead. "I didn't say anything I wasn't supposed to, did I?"

I shook my head. "You were spelled against it. Whatever you took from the embassy. Carlos doesn't know."

"That tracks." Kalene nodded. "You know Ivan. He never misses a beat. He was afraid something like this might happen. He even called me and reminded me to chew the gum. And I still forgot."

"Why didn't he go?" Trish was not a big Ivan fan. "Seriously, if he knew the danger, why'd he put your neck on the line?"

"I volunteered," Kalene said.

Trish bent closer to the front seat. "What were you doing there anyway? What was the mission? What was so important?"

"Trish!

"What? I know I'm not part of your secret club. But I think we both deserve a debrief. What the heck was it all about?"

"You know I can't tell you," Kalene said. "I'm not even sure if I can tell Constance. It's between me and Ivan."

"Fine," Trish said sourly. "Be that way."

Kalene couldn't seem to stand the teenage angst seething from the backseat. "It's nothing really—just something Ivan said we needed. I don't know why. Seriously though, don't worry about it. Nothing to do with you."

"Wait. Are you saying you don't know the Faction's motivation for spying on vampires?"

"Why would I?"

"Because you were, uh, spying on them." In the rearview, Trish rolled her green eyes again. "Listen, you two, I don't mean to pry but—"

I called Trish out. "You totally mean to pry."

"You're right. I do. Sue me." She held up her hands. "Hear me out, though. And this is a question for both of you. Why do y'all let Ivan call the shots?"

"Cause he's our leader," Kalene said.

"Who made him leader? I thought he dealt with recruitment or whatever."

"Well, yeah, he has the register," Kalene agreed. "But it's not his only job. It's not like he has to recruit. He gets the names. Constance is the only hard case I'm aware of."

The register was a spelled book—not to be confused with a spellbook. It listed the members of the Faction. When a new name appeared inside it, Ivan "recruited" them to join.

It was a destiny thing. A person's name inside the book guaranteed membership.

Ivan didn't have a lot to do except seek these people out.

Holding the book was Ivan's only official duty. Just like mine was being the secret keeper. The book of secrets was hidden in my purse.

I saw Trish's point. What made Ivan our leader? I'd never thought to question it... until now.

"Why *is* he our leader?" I asked Kalene.

"Constance," she said, "you're not really buying into Trish's thinking, are you?"

"I'm serious," I said. "It was you two in the beginning. You and Ivan, that is. I assume you let him take the lead.

And as others joined, no one ever stopped and asked for a vote, did they? That's not how it should work, right?"

"It's not like there's a manual." Kalene struggled. "But you've been to our meetings. We all have a say. Ivan's not a dictator."

"Except in covert affairs," Trish pointed out, under her breath but loud enough.

Kalene closed her eyes and swallowed whatever she wanted to say.

"What?" Trish asked her.

"You'll never understand."

"What won't I understand?"

Kalene cleared her throat. "Listen. I know the three of us have a lot of crazy in our own family histories. More than most. We've chosen to deal with it in our own ways. The Faction isn't just *like* a family to me. It is my family. Ivan is my brother. I'd do anything for him. If you spent more time with him, you'd understand."

"I've spent more than enough time with Ivan," Trish said. "No thank you."

"See. Like I said. You'll never understand. I can explain and explain and explain. You won't listen to me. You never have and you never will."

"Whatever you say." Trish made a face, then she lay back down on the seat. "Y'all wake me up when we're close."

It wasn't long before she was snoring, her jaw slack and her mouth open.

"I know you two are friends," Kalene said, "but you shouldn't involve her in Faction business. It's your job to keep our secrets, and you aren't doing much of that, are you?"

First Trish, now Kalene struck me with hard-hitting

facts. "You're right. I don't know how to explain it. I guess before last night, I was just feeling left out."

"It's not like that," Kalene said. "You've been busy. We get it. We do. Ivan talks about you a lot at the meetings you miss. We understand. Caring for you mom is a full-time job."

"Okay, so you promise you're not hiding some Faction secret? We aren't going to war with the vampires, are we? Cause if we are, I don't think I should be helping them solve some mystery."

Kalene looked back at the sleeping Trish. "I'll tell you, but I think maybe I should spell Trish's ears first."

"She's asleep," I said. "I think that's good enough."

"You don't think it's necessary to keep our secret?"

"Whether it is or not, I think she'd kill you if she ever found out you spelled anything of hers. I'm trying to save your life here."

Kalene smiled. "Fair enough."

"So, why were you at the Vampiric Embassy?"

Kalene leaned over. She was on the cusp of whispering something when her face went completely blank.

"That's odd," she said.

"What is?"

"I really don't remember why he sent me there."

6

THE QUIET HOUSE

Mom was just getting out of bed when I got to Gran's house. It was nearly dinner time. Being mostly nocturnal for the past few decades, she struggled to sleep at night. Instead, she stayed up late binging the numerous TV shows she'd missed and eating all sorts of junk food.

We kept a list on the fridge, spanning everything from the Golden Girls to The Walking Dead and sitcoms in between. Nearly half of them were crossed off, some twice—she was particular to *The Office* and *Charmed,* crossing through them three times.

Mom's real name was Serena Young Campbell. In her youth, Gran had called her Rena.

Like me, her hair was blonde. Her eyes blue. She had her father's small nose and his short stature where I was built more like Gran, big boned—what Gran called sturdy.

Mom rarely ventured out. She rarely brushed her hair. She had to be coaxed into the shower.

She understood me, but I wasn't sure she understood who I was. Or where she was.

I found her puttering around the kitchen, making toast, her magic doing most of the work.

The toast popped out of the toaster and landed on a plate which zoomed over my head to the table. Then the refrigerator door opened and a stick of butter flew to meet it.

I had to swerve before the grape jelly plowed into my midsection.

Magic only works when you need it most. Mom's magic worked in the most basic sense, to keep her physiological needs met.

I couldn't fix her. It took all of me to keep her safe. Hopefully she felt the love I sent her way.

Mom hovered over the cutlery drawer, looking confused. With a eureka-ish smile, she brandished a steak knife.

"Butter knife." I pointed them out. "This one's for cutting meat, not butter."

She nodded, her smile fading, and put the steak knife away. With the preferred utensil, she sat down at the table. The butter melted as she slid the cold knife through it.

Magic.

Whether it *needed* to help her in this way was open for debate.

I knew she wasn't doing it on purpose. To her, this was just how the world worked. And this was why she couldn't get out much.

Creel Creek wasn't entirely inhabited by paranormals, though it seemed the people here always had some sort of connection. Some reason to have roots here, whether they were part Fae or lost their connection to magic several ancestors ago.

"She wants to know if you want some," Brad, mine and Mom's familiar, said.

It wasn't she couldn't speak. She could say a few words

now and then. It was the word choices tripping her up. She didn't like to talk if she could help it, preferring instead to use our universal translator.

Brad nibbled on dry cat food from the dish beside the garage door. He looked like an overweight raccoon with long whiskers and beady black eyes hidden in the bands above his mask. His ears pricked up like a terrier's.

He gave me a nod when I came inside but hadn't said anything—at least not to me.

At the moment, we weren't exactly on the best of terms.

It had everything to do with him lying to me since the moment we met. I trusted him. I trusted him with everything. With every thought. With every memory. He knew everything about me, and he'd held back everything about him, telling me I was his first witch when I was just one of so many, including my mother, who he'd abandoned when she needed him most.

Sure, he'd done the right thing in the end. He'd helped me get Mom back. But one right doesn't outweigh his so many terrible wrongs. And I wasn't going to let him forget that I'd saved him once too.

In my mind, we were even. And we were done.

"No thanks." I waved off a piece of toast already hurtling toward my face. It veered around me and back onto Mom's plate once more.

I smiled, hoping it looked as encouraging to her as I meant it to be. "Did you sleep well?"

Mom shrugged.

"She sleeps like a rock," Brad said.

I ignored him.

Mom ate in silence, then got up and wandered into the living room. Not long after, the TV flickered on.

Brad sat beside his dish, watching me, watching her. "What?" I asked him.

"Nothing."

"Something."

"Nothing."

"You have any issues?" I asked. "Did she try to run away again?"

He shook his raccoon head. "Nothing like that. It was a quiet night and an even quieter morning."

"Good."

"Have you talked to Dave?" Brad asked.

"I haven't. He was preoccupied last night and busy this morning. I was driving when he called me back. I don't think he wanted our conversation overheard by Trish and Kalene." I regurgitated my answer so fast it hadn't occurred to me to question Brad's question. Until it did. "Why do you ask?"

"Because there's a gleam in your eyes. You're up to something."

"Really?" I scrutinized the raccoon. "There's a *gleam* in my eyes?" I air quoted. "You're one to talk about being up to something."

"It's possible," he said, "that I helped myself to a few of your thoughts."

"Which I've asked you to stop doing. So, if you knew I didn't talk to Dave, why ask?"

"Can't I be interested in current events? I knew you hadn't talked to Dave about the vampires or what you're doing for them. You haven't talked to me about it, either."

"It doesn't involve you."

"It could," he said. "I'd like to help."

"Hey! I wasn't thinking about any of that."

"I might've helped myself to a few of your recent memories too."

I pinched the bridge of my nose. "How am I ever supposed to trust you if you keep doing things like that?"

"You're never going to trust me again," Brad said. "I've already come to terms with it. Now, I'm just trying to help you in any way I can."

"You can help plenty," I said. "I promised Dave I'd be there for dinner tonight. And there's a Faction meeting later."

"Does that mean more babysitting duty for me?"

"You guessed right."

"Constance." Brad's tone was admonishing.

"What?"

"I can do more than that."

"I'm aware," I said. "You be aware of this—whether it was your fault or not, you're part of the reason she's in the state she's in. The least you can do is take care of her from time to time."

"Except it's not the most I could do," Brad said. "I can help you sort out your magic. I can help catch whoever—or whatever—is disappearing people."

"I know. I'm just not ready to accept you help."

"Fine," he pouted. "You should also know I accepted a call on the mirror-phone earlier."

"I've got to go to Dave's tonight."

"She wants you to call her back," Brad said.

"I will... eventually."

7

THE NOT-SO-QUIET HOUSE

The front door was unlocked. I didn't have to dig in my purse for keys. I tried to sneak inside, pushing the door open with barely a whisper at the hinges.

For a second, I thought I might surprise them. Then I heard the rumbling stampede of feet coming down the stairs. Dave's middle child, Elsie, greeted me like we hadn't seen each other in weeks.

It had been two days.

She managed to hear me over the TV in the living room blaring the soundtrack of yet another Disney musical.

Dave added his own music to the mix—the sizzling of meat from the kitchen and humming as he mixed the melodies of two of his favorite hair bands.

Elsie wrapped my waist in a fierce hug. "Constance," she said, "do you wanna play while we wait for dinner?"

"I don't know," I said. "Your dad might need some help."

"No help needed." Dave leaned over the kitchen island so we could see him.

"You sure?" I asked. "It sounded like you need some

help. What song were you singing—*Here I Go Again Pouring Some Sugar On Me?*"

"It's called a mashup. They're big right now. I think." Dave shot me a smile, his mustache bristling. "You're good with venison, right?"

"That depends," I said. "Was it shot or, uh, *acquired* by other means?"

He looked sheepish. "Does it matter?"

"Kinda."

"Fine. It was acquired." He kept a straight face in spite of my horrified one. "I'm kidding. I got it from Mac last month. He had too much."

"Oh, good." I sighed in relief.

"You know, in all my years as a wolf, I've never woken up with leftovers."

My relief was short lived.

Still glued to my hip, Elsie beamed up at me. The gaps in her smile were filling in with permanent teeth. "We're going to have chicken tenders. I don't like eating deer."

"Yet," Dave countered.

"Yuck." She stuck her tongue out at him.

I laughed. "So, what are we playing?"

"Trolls," she exclaimed.

"Trolls?" I pictured the little dolls of my youth with their neon hair and bedazzled bellybuttons. But knowing Elsie, this game wouldn't involve something as simple as vintage figurines.

"You can be the bridge troll. I'm the mountain troll. And Kacie's a river troll."

"What about Allie?"

"She's watching a movie. She doesn't play *baby* games anymore."

"Is this a baby game?"

"She says it is."

"Cause it is," Allie called from the couch.

"How do you play?" I asked before Elsie could respond to her older sister.

"I'll show you! Let's go upstairs." She tugged at my arm. "It's all set up."

Dave had been watching the interaction with interest.

"Ten minutes," Dave called. "Then we feast." On our way up the stairs, I heard him mumbling something about chicken nuggets.

We found Kacie, the youngest, upstairs in the room she shared with Elsie. She was holding a blue thermos in one hand and drawing a picture on their marker board with the other.

She smiled at us, then her face fell. "You forgot to turn into stone."

Elsie slapped her forehead. "Sorry!" The little girl went rigid. Out of the side of her mouth, she said, "Can you turn off the light?"

"Mountain trolls turn into stone in the sunlight," Kacie said, still coloring.

"Oh. Right." I flicked off the light. Their nightlight clicked on. I guess it didn't count as sunlight because Elsie moved freely again.

Kacie eyeballed the marker board. It was hard to make out what she'd been drawing. "I wasn't finished," she complained.

"You can finish later," Elsie told her. "Constance is playing too. She's a mountain troll. Do we have any goats to feed her?"

"Mountain trolls do eat goats," Kacie said matter-of-factly. "I don't have any. But we do have a cow and a pig."

"That's right. Miss Piggy and Bluebell."

Kacie rummaged through their stuffed animals until she found the cow and the Muppet. "They'll have to do."

She handed them to me. "What am I supposed to do with them?"

"Eat them. Duh!"

"And after that?"

She shrugged. "The important thing is not to get tricked into fighting their older brother."

"They have an older brother?"

"Duh!"

"Since when do you say duh?"

"Since you made us watch Full House," Elsie told me.

"Duh," Kacie said.

"We're going to have to work on that," I said.

Ten minutes later, we were downstairs at the dining room table. The girls asked about Washington DC. We talked about the zoo and the pandas. I promised to take them there over summer break.

Dave eyed me. I knew he knew I was holding something —everything—back.

And he hated talking shop at the dinner table, so I couldn't even ask him about the bank robbery featured on the latest episode of *Creel Creek After Dark*.

We were at an impasse—at least until dinner was over.

My phone chimed.

I looked down to see a message from Ivan.

"Anything important?" Dave asked.

"Ivan wants to talk to me before the meeting tonight."

"Before as in now?" Dave raised an eyebrow.

"Pretty much."

He nodded. "Are you going to come back, or are you sleeping at your grandmother's again tonight?"

"I hadn't thought about it."

I had thought about it. I'd thought about it a lot. I wanted to be here with Dave. But every moment here felt like a moment stolen from my mother.

Then every moment with her, with her lack of progress as we watched show after show and movie after movie, felt like wasted moments I could be with Dave.

Things were so complicated. I couldn't bring her here. And they couldn't go there. It wouldn't make sense.

I would always be pulled between the two houses. I was Juliet and Dave my Romeo. Was our love fated for a tragic ending?

"Can you think about it?" Dave asked. "Cause there's something I'd like to talk to you about. Something important. I'd prefer to discuss it without so many tiny ears around."

"My ears aren't tiny," Elsie argued.

"Your ears are perfect," I told her, brushing her hair behind them. She was right. They weren't exactly tiny.

"Well?" Dave brought his hand down on the table, rattling the plates.

The room went quiet.

It was exactly the scenario I'd played in my head, walking down the streets of Washington.

My stomach lurched as I searched for meaning in his words. I didn't like his tone either.

Only a few minutes before, we'd bantered about song mashups. It hadn't taken much to sour the mood—just a text from Ivan.

There was no getting out of the meeting. I couldn't cancel. Not again. Not after everything with Kalene and the mission I'd accepted on the Faction's behalf.

I tried to smile with sad puppy dog eyes, hoping it would

lighten Dave's mood. "Am I allowed to know what you'd like to talk about?"

"Us." Dave looked away from me, shaking his head sadly.

My puppy dog eyes hadn't done the trick.

"Us," I repeated. "What about us?"

"Can you be here tonight or not?"

"I'll try," I said.

Lines formed on Dave's forehead, his frustration with me evident. I couldn't blame him. I was frustrated too. I wanted to know what this was about. I wanted to know now. I didn't want to wait.

Waiting sucks.

But it was Dave. He was worth the wait.

"I mean, I will be here tonight," I said. "Promise."

My promise didn't hold much weight with him.

"Good," he said.

It didn't sound good at all. I couldn't help wondering if I was right and Trish was wrong.

Maybe it was the end.

The end of our relationship.

8

IN WITCH THE FACTION GATHERS

I know I'm not the only person to devote hours of time and study on secret societies.

For me, it happened in the early 2000s—shortly after the movie *The Skulls* came out. This was prior to the miracle of Wikipedia and back when the internet wasn't quite so infinite.

I looked up everything—the Illuminati and The Skull and Bones, the student society which served as the basis for the movie.

Yale was never in the cards for me.

I could never have imagined a secret society was either. And yet, here I was.

Except when I'd gone down the secret society rabbit hole, I pictured meetings in nondescript buildings with hidden passages. I pictured hooded figures with their faces in shadow.

I never pictured this.

If I told my younger self about a secret magical organization known as the Faction, she might not immediately laugh it off as a joke. No, that would happen as soon as I told her their meetings were held at the local hotel bar.

To be more precise—the outdoor courtyard at the Creel Creek Mountain Lodge.

I parked, got out and skirted the main building. With its log construction lobby and green tin roof, it reminded me of Lincoln Logs.

The courtyard maintained the rustic feel. It was a perfect circle, ringed with stone. It had a large fireplace in the center and a waterfall feature on the side opposite from the bar.

Not exactly what I'd pictured for a secret society.

I'd pictured something more like the League of Artemis —the order of shifters Dave belonged to. In their underground den, under large cloaks, their members attended the meetings in their *shifted* form.

Here, it was casual attire and Faction members held extra-large margarita glasses. At the end of the meetings, they dared each other with flaming shots of alcohol—only once had someone set their face on fire.

Luckily, we knew magic.

On my way through the courtyard, I nodded at a few familiar faces.

Ivan was seated a table away from the bar, nearer to the waterfall than I liked to be. While I understood the waterfall helped muffle our words, the constant sound of water falling mixed with having a couple of drinks made my bathroom trips frequent.

I passed through a spell on my way over—Ivan had soundproofed the area for our meeting.

But he hadn't changed anything else. There were numerous heaters outside as the nighttime temperature hovered close to freezing. I was bundled up and wore a knitted beanie to keep my ears warm.

"What are you drinking tonight?" Ivan waved the waitress over.

Ivan was an average guy with average looks. He didn't stand out in a bar. Probably why it took the waitress several minutes to find her way over to us. She looked at me as Ivan already held a glass of whiskey.

"Wine." I shrugged. "Something red."

"Like?" she asked.

"Do you have anything from Armand Vineyards?" My friend Cyrus owned the vineyard outside of town. Even in Creel Creek, their wines were hard to come by.

"I'll check, but I don't think so. If not, is the house red okay? It's a Merlot."

"That's fine." I didn't want to drink. I wanted to get this meeting over with and get away.

I wanted to finish—to start—my dialogue with Dave. In the car, I'd come up with a dozen reasons he should just break up with me and half a dozen reasons he shouldn't. Too bad he was good at math.

The waitress zipped away, taking another order on her way to the bar.

Ivan smiled. "Feels like it's been ages since we got together and talked, just us."

"We talked the other day."

"Yeah, but that was about Kalene and—"

"And you left out a lot of details?"

He winced into the short glass. "Yeah, well, I'm sorry about that."

"Why didn't you tell me you'd already negotiated with Carlos?"

Ivan looked dubious. "We didn't negotiate. He called me before you got there. I merely suggested a solution. And you two agreed to it. I call that a win."

"Isn't it a touch unfair?" I asked. "Almost like you gave me two missions when I agreed to one."

"Or I gave you a really long mission." Ivan thought he was being funny. I hoped the look on my face told him just how funny I thought he was. "You aren't seriously mad about this, are you? You can't be. Constance, I know how you work. I thought for sure you'd be intrigued."

"I am intrigued," I admitted. That was the problem.

"See. I knew you would be."

"I'm also mad," I said. "I have *other* thoughts too. Questions—like why we, the Faction, didn't take this case to begin with?

"Disappearances happen every day. Linking them to something otherworldly is a stretch." It sounded like part of a rehearsed speech. "I'm still unconvinced this is in our purview," Ivan went on. "I'm hoping you'll figure it all out for us."

"Unconvinced?" I scoffed. "You saw Jade's video. It's pretty convincing."

"Videos can be edited," he said. "Summer's going to look it over for us. Jade kind of dropped the whole episode on us unannounced."

"It doesn't change the fact that Kara Huber is missing."

"It doesn't mean it happened when she was checking her mail." Ivan swirled the ice in his whiskey. "Have you asked your boyfriend? Maybe he knows where she went."

"Not yet," I answered. "But Ivan, what if she did disappear? Where would she go? Maybe the shadow realm?"

He shrugged. "Hard to say."

"Aren't you curious? You don't want to at least help figure this out?"

It didn't seem like a loaded question, but Ivan shied away from it, turning his attention to the bar. "I, uh—I'll be honest here," he said. "I looked into it a bit. You'll see—sooner rather than later—the trail runs cold. It's like a new mystery with every missing person."

"Why didn't you bring it up before?"

He faced me again, his eyebrows knotted with skepticism. "Why didn't I bring it up with you? Are you serious? You know why. Come on! Your only concern has been your mother. I commend you on that. I do. I really do. It's why I wasn't sure if you'd take on the mantle without an extra nudge. And don't worry, if you can't solve it in a few months, somebody else will give it a try. Then someone else and so on and so forth."

I brushed the response away. "So, you aren't going to help me then?"

I wanted a straight answer.

I didn't think I was going to get one. We sat in silence when the waitress returned with my wine.

Finally, Ivan sighed. "I'm not."

I wasn't sure I heard him correctly. "Did you say you're not?"

"There's actually another reason I called this meeting tonight." He took a deep breath. "I guess I might as well tell you now. See, my days here in Creel Creek are numbered. There are too many places I'm needed. I've got a list of twenty names to recruit. Honestly, I've stayed here too long already. I got too comfortable."

"You're—you're leaving?"

He nodded into his glass, then took a sip.

"When?"

"In a week or so." He shrugged. "I can't get into specifics because I don't know them yet. I'm still waiting on things to get ironed out."

"What about us—the Faction? How will you send out orders?"

"These magical devices called phones. Oh, and someone at DARPA invented email a while back. Maybe you've heard of it."

I rolled my eyes. "What about the podcast? Are you still doing it?"

"Video calls," he said.

"Wow. It sounds like all your bases are covered."

"Not all of them. There's a reason I asked you to come early tonight." His eyes searched the bar again. "Creel Creek is basically the home of the Faction. I want you to be my eyes and ears while I'm gone."

"Not Kalene?"

"Kalene's blunder proved to me I couldn't trust her with something like this."

I heard his words but they didn't ring true. Ivan had trusted Kalene through thick and thin. One mistake shouldn't undo that. "I'm not exactly sure I understand what you're asking of me."

"All I need is for you to say yes."

"I, uh, let me think about it," I said.

Still, my insides were squirming. I wanted to say no. It felt like a trick—like when Halitosis Hal spelled my phone using the ruse of putting his number in it.

"Sure." Ivan nodded. "Think about it. I trust you, Constance Campbell. I trust you understand your place in the Faction. Let's not forget what the Faction's done for you."

"What has it done?" I took a swallow of wine.

"Without *our* help, I doubt you'd have gotten your mother out of the grip of that familiar. What was her name again?"

"Morgana." I nearly slung the glass of wine in his face. It

would've been a waste of adequate wine. Most definitely the house red.

Ivan was trying to manipulate me for some reason.

"Right, Morgana," he said.

We struggled to make small talk for a few more minutes. Then it struck me. Ivan wasn't even there. Not when we fought Morgana.

Where was he?

Before I could ask, Ivan's eyes lit up as Slate's tall frame hunkered down beside us.

At the bar, Kalene, Lauren Whittaker, and Summer Shields were ordering drinks. The meeting was about to start.

In non-exact words, Ivan ran through everything about his soon to be departure. We wound down with a debrief of what happened at the Vampiric Embassy.

Afterward, while Ivan chatted up Slate at the bar, Lauren and Kalene tried their hand at karaoke, which left me alone with Summer.

Summer's short red hair looked fiery in the glow of the candlelight at our table. Shadows danced along her pointy features.

As her alter-ego Athena Hunter, Summer hosted the *Creel Creek After Dark* podcast. She and Ivan took part in it, mixing truth with fantasy, making for an entertaining podcast, and keeping their cohost, Jade, mostly in the dark.

Summer was a former nemesis of mine turned confidant and friend.

I leaned close and whispered, "Does he seem different to you?"

"In what way?"

"I don't know." I shrugged. "Every way. The Ivan of a few months ago would've jumped at the chance to help investigate a magical crime. He basically shoved this one off on me."

"I noticed," she said.

"He also seems to have taken a keen interest in vampires."

"Has he?" She scowled. "Maybe he's just preoccupied with his own mission."

"Maybe," I said. "I just wish we knew what that mission is."

She let that sit a moment. "You know, Ivan's not the only person acting different."

"Who else?" I counted the heads at the bar. Ivan, Lauren, Kalene, and Slate, along with some regulars.

"None of them," she said. "It's Jade. She's acting, well, she's acting odd."

"How so?" Odd and Jade Gerwig went hand in hand.

Summer sighed. "You know what I mean—odd for Jade. She's stopped asking me about magic. I swear she's not even speculating anymore. It's like she knows."

"Maybe she does. It's not hard to put two and two together. I thought y'all were on to us way before After Dark Con."

"It's more than that." Summer shook her head, made a face, and finally found the words. "It's like she knows magic. What I mean is, it's like she knows as much as we do. Maybe more. And how she got her hands on that video she brought in yesterday, I have no clue. I swear the Jade Gerwig I used to know is a thing of the past."

9

BEFORE SLEEP

I wrestled with a thousand competing thoughts. It wasn't like I knew what Dave was going to say. Not really. But a part of me was convinced it did.

For a moment, I considered turning around, going to back to the bar and having another drink. Or six.

It wasn't like this was my first rodeo. I'd had feelings like this dozens of times before. It happened with Mark, my ex-husband. Something inside me knew he was cheating on me. Then there was Barry, my other ex-something or other. I'd known he wanted to end things well before our trip to Vegas.

At least Dave was brave enough to talk about his feelings. He wasn't going to write a note or a text.

My feelings were still hurt from my first boyfriend—Chad—whose best friend passed me a note in the hallway.

"Chad gave me this," he said with the nonchalance of a seventh grader.

What I thought was going to be highlights of Chad's fifth period ended up being a few words that broke my heart.

I'm dumping you.

I couldn't help wondering, was Dave about to break my extremely breakable heart?

Unlike a few hours before, the house was quiet and dark. The front door was locked. I used my key, slipped off my shoes, and trudged up the stairs in socks.

A nightlight in the hallway illuminated the carpet underneath it but not much more. The bedroom door was cracked, nearly shut, and there was no light coming from the room.

Did I really stay out so late?

If this talk was so important, why hadn't he waited up for me?

I pushed the door, expecting to find Dave asleep and giving serious thought to leaving and going to Gran's house to check in on Mom. But I found him sitting up in bed, a tablet on his chest. He was reading.

Beside him, sprawled out like she was making a snow angel in the sheets, was Kacie. The little girl was conked out, her feet in the middle of what was usually my spot.

"She's been having nightmares," Dave whispered.

"For how long?" It was such an odd question to ask him. But the truth was I didn't know whether these nightmares started last weekend or if they'd been around a lot longer. I'd missed so much lately because of Mom.

"A month or so." He set the tablet aside.

My heart sank. The reality of the havoc—the strain—the past few months had caused on our relationship was evident here in this moment.

I wasn't sure I was prepared for the moments to come.

"She wouldn't even try to go to bed by herself tonight." Dave brushed hair off her cheek. "Lots of trouble this weekend with her cousins. Jared said she basically didn't get to sleep until after midnight. I've heard of sleep regressions, but honestly, I thought we were way past this."

"That's awful," I said.

"Let me get her tucked in bed. I'll be right back."

Kacie didn't stir as he scooped her up in his arms.

Dave was built like a rock climber, lean with more prominent muscles in his shoulders and chest. How he maintained such a physique with a diet of sugary cereal, pizza, and burgers was a bigger mystery than any I'd ever helped solve.

While Dave insisted it was because he worked out in the mornings before work—I'd never seen him do more than a few pushups—my theory was it had something to do with the *other* side of him. This past weekend he'd spent his nights chasing down deer in the foothills of the Blue Ridge Mountains. A monthly jaunt through the mountains at top speed had to be good for the metabolism.

He returned to the room and told a robot overlord to turn on the lamp. There was a chime and the lamp on the nightstand illuminated a stack of books, Dave's tablet with hundreds more books, and the last portrait of his family before his wife died of cancer. In the picture, she had a head scarf which only seemed to accentuate the beauty in her eyes and smile.

Dave slid into his side of the bed and nodded toward the empty spot beside him. "I thought you were staying the night."

I was still standing and still unsure what he wanted to talk about. "Am I?"

"I just assumed..."

"I'm here because you wanted to talk," I said.

"Right." He patted the bed a couple times. "You can still sit down."

I took the edge of the bed, leaving a large gap between us. "Better?"

"Slightly," he chuckled. "Are you all right? What happened tonight at your meeting? You never told me how it went in DC either. I assume Kalene's okay?"

"It went," I said.

"All right." He sighed. "I guess I deserve this for the way I acted before. I'm sorry I got testy about you coming back tonight. It was just a rough weekend. Barely got any sleep. And I wanted to see you."

"You said you wanted to talk... about us."

"I did—I do." He looked away, and the part of me that thought it knew everything was suddenly triumphant. Not in a good way.

"I knew it," I said. "I just knew it."

"You knew what?"

"You're going to break up with me."

"I'm going to what?"

The ball was already rolling, and I couldn't stop the words from slipping out of my stupid mouth. "It's fine. I understand. It's been a rocky six months. We barely see each other anymore. And when we do, we aren't alone. The girls are always there. And if I do stay over, I'm tired. I can't help Mom's up all night, and I feel like I have to be there with her.

"You need someone who can put you and your family first. That's just not me right now. What we had was great. And I'll cherish the time I got to spend with you and with the girls. If you want, I'll talk to them. I'll figure something out."

"Can I stop you right now?" he asked.

I took a deep breath. "Sure. I think I said what I need to."

"Well, what I wanted to talk about wasn't that." The lines

around Dave's eyes crinkled as he grinned. "Seriously? You thought I was going to break up with you?"

"It makes sense."

"It doesn't." He shook his head. "Constance, we all go through rough patches. Life throws us curve ball after curve ball. I do think the last few months have been hard. You've been swinging away at them while I've been taking the strikes."

"Could we not with the baseball analogies?"

"Sorry." He smiled. "Just let me finish what I was going to say before you try to talk me into breaking up with you again."

"That's fair." I smiled too—only because his was infectious.

"This weekend got me thinking," he said. "If you can get away for a couple of days. If I can get away for a couple of days. Then why can't we both get away?"

"What are you saying?"

"If you're free in three weeks, I'd like to book us a condo. Just me and you and the beach for a few days. Imogene and Jared will take the girls. I assume Brad and maybe Summer could help out with your mom? Trish can take your shift."

"I don't know. That's a big ask."

"Summer helping out with your mom?"

"No. Trish and the store."

He laughed. "She owes me a favor."

"You're serious?" I asked him.

"About the favor?"

I shook my head. "About the beach. About us getting away together."

"Of course."

My heart was beating so fast. How had I thought this perfect man was going to break up with me? I scooted across the space between us, making it disappear. I kissed his kiss-able cheek.

"Now, will you tell me about DC and the vampires?"

"Just the one vampire," I said. "And I'll tell you about it. But can we do something else first?"

THE LAMP WAS OFF, but the room hadn't completely faded to black. A sliver of moonlight peeked through the curtains. It cut across Dave's chest, a reminder of the claim it had on him.

Dave and the moon were in the longest of long-term relationships. He would be a werewolf for the rest of his life. And no matter where he went, he couldn't hide from the moon or its magical hold over him.

While the moon wasn't a source of magical energy, it did have magical significance. Tonight, it was nearly full but waning. In a few weeks, at the crescent moon, witches around the world would circle and perform their own rituals.

I'd be one of them, trying yet again to help Mom reconnect her body, mind, and spirit.

With my fingers twisting through the hairs on Dave's chest, I gave a rundown of my weekend activity. He did the same.

Dave hadn't been at work when the bank robbery happened. However, he did oversee the arrest of the suspect, who he didn't want to name for some reason. The man was currently being held in the county jail.

"What do you think?" Dave whispered. "Any link to those disappearances?"

"You never talked to me about those either," I said.

"Not true. I told you about Kara Huber, the psychic."

"Did you?"

"You were preoccupied. It was right around the time your mom started using magic."

"Oh."

"There was no evidence of foul play. She was just gone. You'd think if anyone could see something bad coming, it was her. Granted, most everyone thought she was a fraud. Her powers couldn't compare to Willow's."

"What about the others?"

"You know I listen to the podcast too," he said. "Half the time, they don't know what's what. I'll give them people in Creel Creek do disappear. Usually, it's nothing sinister. Some are known to leave when they see something here they don't like. Some go off to other worlds. Take your grandmother for example. As for elsewhere—the list your vampire friend made up—I can't speak to them."

"He's not my friend."

"Do you think he's on to something?"

"It's hard to say. As for your suspect, I can't imagine he'll disappear from jail. He didn't happen to mention if he'd seen a vampire around, did he?"

"No vampires. Just says it didn't happen. It was all a dream. We've proved to him otherwise, but he won't believe us. Mac's convinced he's going for the insanity plea."

"Mac's not really an outside of the box thinker. I still don't understand why you promoted him to detective."

"As a detective, he doesn't need to think outside the box. I need levelheaded and pragmatic, and he's those in spades."

"So, what do you think?" I asked. "Do you believe the suspect was dreaming?"

"I believe he believes it. I don't think he's crazy. I just

think he's had it rough—a rough few years. I just wish we could rule everything else out before taking it to the district attorney."

"How could you rule everything out?"

"Well," he looked down at me, his cheek scratching against the top of my head, "I could use some help of the magical variety."

"I'm in," I said. "Just let me know what you need me to do."

"Look in his head and see if any of the crazy he's talking is real, or if he's lying like Mac seems to think."

"Dave," I craned my neck so I could see him, even in the darkness. "I don't have that kind of magic. I can't read someone's thoughts."

"You don't. But you know *someone* who does, right? Someone who can read minds..." Dave cringed—and for good reason.

My jaw clenched. "You mean Brad."

10

PAWSOME PUNISHMENT

No matter how many times I'd been to Dave's office —and it had been many—I never felt comfortable there. Whether it was to meet him for lunch, drop off something he'd forgotten, or even to help with a case, something about being at the sheriff's office made my insides squirm.

I parked outside and scoped out the parking lot. For now, the coast looked clear. "You can stop hiding."

Brad clambered up onto the center console. "How are we going to play this?"

"Play what?" I asked.

"Reading this guy's mind," Brad said.

"Oh... I figured I'd go in while you go around to the back where they do the interviews. Or you can stay in the car. I can leave it on so you don't get too hot."

"It doesn't work like that."

"You don't get hot?"

"No," he growled, frustrated. "I can't read someone's mind from right here."

"You can read mine from anywhere."

"We have a connection. It's different."

"All right, then we'll go with the other plan. If you get out now, no one will see you cut around the building."

"Is there a window?" Brad asked.

"I don't think so. If memory serves, there's a camera in the room. No window."

"A camera? No, a camera won't work either."

I didn't see what the big deal was. "Why don't you make a suggestion?"

"Constance, to see into someone's mind, I have to actually see them. At the very least, I have to look them in the eyes. Eyes are the windows into the soul. I thought you knew this."

"I might've... at some point." I grunted, shoving my door open. "I guess you're coming inside with me."

"Couldn't there be normals inside? How many people in there know you're a witch?"

"Almost everyone... I think."

"It's mostly shifters, right?"

"Mostly," I agreed.

"I want a number," Brad said.

I thought a moment. "There're a couple that aren't paranormal," I said. "Who knows, they might not even be in there. It *is* the lunch hour. I can call Dave and ask."

"Either way, I think you need a plan. Just in case."

As helpful as Brad liked to think he was, he could be literally the opposite. I channeled Trish. "How about I wear you as a hat?"

"Is that a Davy Crockett reference? A real raccoon would take offense."

"Good thing you aren't." I sighed, exasperated. "What do you suggest?"

"Well, as vulgar as the Davy Crockett thing is, it's not really a bad idea."

"All right. I'll make you look like something else. I don't know. I could make you a purse."

"Ha."

"I don't know. A pet? Except if I was carrying around a cat, I think they'd still probably bat an eye. It's not exactly typical to bring a live animal into the office. Unless..."

"Unless what?"

"Unless it's a new puppy—they wouldn't think it was weird, but there's a hundred percent chance they'd come over and pet you."

"There's another problem," Brad said. "You can't spell me to look like a puppy. Your magic doesn't work on me. This is who I am in this world, magically speaking."

I rubbed my temples. "You know I didn't ask for your help, right? It's Dave who wants it. I'll just tell him you couldn't make it."

"I'm trying to teach you something here. Something about magic."

The shtick might've worked on me before, but it didn't now. "Then teach," I said.

"You can't change my appearance. But you can change what people see. You could make me all but invisible. It'd be a complex spell. Honestly, I'm not sure if your magic's up for it."

"Then what do you suggest?"

"I guess we'll have to go with the puppy plan," Brad said grudgingly. "Make them believe that's what I am. They'll see what you want them to see."

"Sounds good to me." I didn't move. It sounded like a good plan, but there were other issues. I hadn't made up a spell in months. I was out of practice.

"Make up the rhyme," Brad said. "Practice it. Then we'll go."

> "Ears floppy. Tufts of fur.
> Breath for which there is no cure.
> Mischievous and innocent, at the same time.
> Something so cute should be a crime.
> If they aren't a witch like me,
> A puppy they will see."

THE INSIDE of the building reminded me of a startup more than it did any police station I'd seen on television. There were cubicles in the pit, offices along the walls, and a kitchenette in the break room.

What set it apart was the storage closets. They held a lot more than office supplies. There were gun cabinets, a whole room full of evidence, and two holding cells were hidden away in the bowels of the building.

I noticed a few familiar faces, but there were several I couldn't put names to. It seemed like every officer on duty was milling about at the station, not on patrol or elsewhere.

While Dave usually made a point to hire paranormals or at least those aware we exist, there were exceptions. One was a new hire, the deputy who replaced Willow. We missed her in Creel Creek. She'd traded us for the Florida heat and the alligators.

Willow's replacement, Lydia Pickford, was put together and professional. She was everything you could want in a deputy. Dave had no choice but to hire her, despite her lack of paranormal understanding. I only questioned how she found herself in Creel Creek to begin with.

Lydia's hair was slicked back in a tight bun. Her uniform was neat and pressed. What stood out was her bright red lipstick. "Is that a Labradoodle?" she exclaimed, bounding across the pit at us.

A few other officers took notice and gathered around. I held Brad out for them to see. "Watch out. He's still got those razor-sharp puppy teeth."

"Are you suggesting I bite her?" Brad's voice could only be heard by a witch.

Don't you dare bite her.

"Oh, puppy breath." Lydia stuck her nose in Brad's face.

I was surprised the spell had worked so well. What they saw was a ball of chocolatey brown curls with a beard and dark eyes hidden behind the fur on his brow. To make things easier, I'd thought the puppy to be about the same size as Brad as a raccoon.

More deputies arrived, taking turns squishing Brad's face and stroking his back.

"I feel violated here," Brad said.

"He's a chunky fella," a deputy said, scratching Brad behind the ears.

"Watch it, pal." The puppy version somehow growled from deep in his chest.

The deputy withdrew his hand quickly and laughed. "Must've been something I said."

"It's not what you say but how you say it," Lydia sing-songed. "He doesn't speak puppy. "You've got to speak puppy. See. Now, he knows I'm not a threat." She gave Brad a big kiss on the jaw.

"This might be your worst idea yet," Brad thought.

And weirdly my most satisfying. I could get used to this.

"Does that mean we can be partners again?"

Maybe one day. I sighed.

"What a cutie," Lydia came up for air. "I just want to take him home with me."

"I don't think the girls would approve," I told Lydia. "He's a surprise. I brought him by to show Dave before I take him to meet them. Is he around?"

"Oh, right." It didn't seem to have occurred to her—or anyone else for that matter—how odd it was I'd brought a puppy into the station.

Mac's office was empty. Dave's was out of sight, in another part of the building, behind a receptionist. "You know," he said, "I think they were about to interview that perp."

"I'll take you," Lydia said.

Brad's thoughts echoed in my mind. "You realize you're going to have to keep up this charade, right? Dave might have to bring in puppy pictures from time to time."

Crap. You're right.

"Or you could perform a memory charm."

"I could," I accidently said, rather than think.

"You could what?" Lydia asked.

"Oh, nothing."

I was already trying to think of something that rhymed with memory. We turned a corner. A deputy was ushering a tall, lanky man down the hallway.

At the sight of the man, the air rushed out of my lungs. It took a moment to register why.

"It's Doug," I said more to myself than anyone else.

"Who?" Brad asked.

"Doug," I said again.

Recognizing his name, the man looked our way. He didn't seem to remember me, or register the faux

Labradoodle in my arms. His dark, sunken eyes brushed past mine.

The deputy guided him into the interrogation room, and they disappeared behind the door.

"He looks haunted," Brad said.

Yeah but by what?

11

THOUGHTS OF THE THOUGHTLESS

Dave was waiting in the adjacent room with Detective Michael 'Mac' Mackenzie.

The red-headed fox shifter tipped his head in my direction before his jaw went slack and his eyes nearly crossed. The sight of Brad, the Labradoodle, in my arms had him totally befuddled. "I thought you were bringing your raccoon."

Lydia, who was nearly out the door, spun around. "Wait —" her eyes lit up "—did he just say you have a raccoon? That's... that's..."

"Nonsense." I put a calming hand on her shoulder. Later, I would most definitely remove this memory from her brain. "What kind of person owns a raccoon?"

"A witch." Dave elbowed Mac hard in the ribs and gave the shifter a hard look. Dave had to be equally confused about Brad but somehow held it together.

I realized, too late, the spell had worked on everyone not like me—including shifters and werewolves.

"I was teasing Mac earlier," Dave said. "Told him you might bring in a new pet."

"And he really thought I'd get the girls a raccoon?" I laughed.

Lydia punched Mac in the shoulder. "Goofball!" she said. "You'll believe anything if it doesn't come from the lips of a suspect."

Mac went from rubbing his side to his shoulder. His face turned the color of his hair. "Don't you have somewhere to be?" he asked her.

"Oh, right." Lydia replied, then bent down to give Brad one last pat. "It was nice meeting you... You never told us his name."

"Fluffers," I made up on the spot with a laugh.

"Laugh it up," Brad sneered.

"I guess you got me, boss," Mac said, as Lydia strode out of the room. "But I could swear she has a raccoon. I think I've seen it before."

"That's cause she does." Dave peered down at Brad. "This is magic. You can tell if you try. There's something not quite right about this dog."

Mac nodded, looked skeptically down at Brad, then gave him a pat on the head. "Seems like a puppy to me."

I couldn't help but laugh. "He's your best detective?"

"The best I've got," Dave said. "Mac, why don't you go in the next room and get started. I'll be in shortly."

With Mac and Lydia out of the room, Dave wanted answers. "What's with the dog?"

"It's Brad."

"I know it's Brad. I'm asking why."

"Would it be better to bring a raccoon in the building?"

Dave pinched the bridge of his nose. "He couldn't stay outside?"

I explained the predicament, including the fact we'd all have to cozy up in the interrogation room.

"You don't think the suspect might find it odd if I bring my girlfriend and her pet into the interrogation?" Dave asked.

I didn't answer because I had questions of my own. "Suspect?" I scoffed. "Why didn't you tell me it was Doug?"

Dave grimaced. "I was afraid if I told you who it was, you wouldn't agree to help."

"More like I wouldn't have waited until today."

"Really?" Dave raised an eyebrow. "You do remember this guy held a gun to your head, right?"

"It wasn't aimed at me," I said. "It was to the side. Plus, he was coerced. Hal had him spellbound."

It had been over two years since I'd moved to Creel Creek and nearly that long since my short stint working at the grocery store. One day, a warlock had used Doug to threaten my life, then later, used him to get Dave out of the picture.

Doug shot Dave with the same gun, using a silver bullet, albeit sterling silver.

Doug was still a teenager when all this happened. The courts don't exactly allow things like possession by magic to be entered in as evidence, but Dave did his best and got him tried as a juvenile, with a lighter sentence.

"Still," Dave said, "I didn't think you'd be so enthusiastic. The boy in there doesn't understand what happened to him back then. What's worse is he doesn't seem to understand what happened to him the other day. That's why I need you here. But putting you in the next room? I'm not sure that's going to fly."

"You could strengthen the spell," Brad suggested.

"Don't worry." I thought it over. "I'm going to make it so Doug doesn't notice us at all. The way he looked out there, strengthening the spell to make the two of us invisible shouldn't be too hard. Just make sure to smooth things out with Mac."

"Not a problem." Dave rolled his eyes.

———————

THE PAST TWO years hadn't been kind to Doug. He was gaunt, bone thin except a slight belly. He had scraggily tattoos on his forearms and neck. The worst part was his eyes. They were as vacant as the sea.

Across the table, Mac was the opposite—as animated as I'd ever seen him. He was in his element. Maybe Dave was right about his skill as a detective.

"I'm going to ask you for what, the sixth time, now—why don't you go ahead and confess? Lay it all out there for us, and I promise we'll go easy on ya."

Or not.

Doug wouldn't look him in the eye. "I already told you there's nothing to confess."

"Right. Right." Mac gave Dave a knowing look. "And you're sure you don't want an attorney present today?"

"Didn't do me any good the last time," Doug said. "Way I see it, you've made your mind up. I'm going back in no matter what I say or do."

"While that's true," Mac said, "I want to remind you this time it won't be juvie. This'll be the real deal. You're looking at prison time, son. You should just confess."

"I can't confess."

"You're just going to sit there and say nothing?"

"I'll answer your questions. It's not going to hurt me to answer your questions—when I know I didn't do it."

"All right." Mac scrubbed his face and smiled. "So, if you didn't do it then why do you think you're here?"

"Cause you *believe* I robbed the bank."

"It's not *we believe* you robbed the bank," Mac said, not unkindly. "Doug, we know you robbed the bank. We have video. We have witnesses. Your fingerprints are everywhere fingerprints can be. They're on the counter. They're on the money we found in your house. They're on the gun under your bed. The same one used in the robbery."

"I didn't do it," Doug said with conviction.

"Okay. But you can see we have a mountain of proof. The only reason we're entertaining you in here today is cause the sheriff here would like to know why—why you did it when it was plain to everyone you were bound to get caught. Son, you didn't even wear a mask."

"I didn't do it!" Doug was finally indignant enough to sit up. He looked around the room, just now taking in Dave, who was standing behind us, leaning on the wall. Doug's eyes bounced off me and Brad. To him, it looked like an empty chair, ready for Dave.

"I'm spitballing here," Mac said. "Let's assume you thought about robbing the bank once or twice. We all do it. You ever go in the bank and see all that money and think there's no reason I can't take it? I mean, after all, it's insured. It's not like anyone loses. No one except the FDIC and who even are they anyway?" Mac leaned over the table. "What do you say, Doug? You ever have those thoughts? Am I the only one?"

"Maybe." The boy shrugged.

"Just maybe?"

"What do you want me to say, man? Of course I have. Everyone in town knows what I did. They won't even hire me to flip burgers. Money's tight right now, ya know?"

"I get it." Mac nodded. "How are you employed these days, Doug?"

"Day labor, sometimes." He looked away again. "Odd jobs. Construction, but I got fired."

"Why's that?"

"Boss kept saying I was too scrawny. Said I couldn't lift enough."

"So you quit?"

He shook his head. "No, I was fired. I got pissed off, hopped in a bulldozer, and took out part of a house."

"Huh, they didn't call us."

"It was getting torn down anyway," Doug said.

"Ah. Still, I bet that felt good. Kind of like robbing a bank might feel good. Or so you thought... Did it feel good to rob the bank?"

"I don't know."

"You don't know if it felt good or?"

"I don't know cause I didn't rob the bank."

"We're just throwing out hypotheticals. None of this means you actually robbed the bank. Even though we know you did. Right now, I'm just wondering if you were having these thoughts. And maybe if you were having them a little more than let's say, I might have them."

"I was," Doug agreed. "I thought about it lots of times. It doesn't mean I robbed the place."

"No, the video means you robbed the place. We just want to know why. And why do it in a way bound to get you caught? When's the last time you had a thought like this?"

"I don't know. A week ago. Maybe."

"You mean you planned it for a whole week?" Mac smiled. "And it went so well. Imagine if you gave it a month."

"I didn't plan anything!"

"Why were you there if you weren't planning on robbing the place?"

"I had a check to cash. I don't know. All I remember is

going to bed, thinking about cashing the check. When I woke up, you and the cops were outside my door."

"Sorry for waking you." Mac smirked at Dave.

"What do you think?" Dave asked me.

It was apparent Mac thought the kid was lying or confused or high. Honestly, in any other town, in any other situation, I'd probably think the same.

But this was Creel Creek, and I was on a mission.

There wasn't much behind Doug's eyes, and when he spoke about the robbery, there was truth—an innocence—in his tone.

I lifted Brad up in my arms. "What do you see?"

"There's not much going on inside his head," Brad said. "But I don't think he's lying."

He's not? You mean he's not thinking about the robbery?

"It's not *just* his thoughts," Brad said. "He's not lying because the robbery's not a memory he possesses. Well, that's not exactly true. It's not in his living memories anyway. When he tries to remember, there's a flash of something gray and upside down—almost like the memory of a dream."

So, he did dream it?

"It seems so."

Then why can't he remember?

"Dreams don't make lasting memories," Brad said.

I tried to explain to Dave and Mac, who was having none of it.

"It makes sense if you think about it," I said. "Dreams are just a byproduct—they're what you get when your mind is sorting through memories, tossing away what's not important."

"That's what the scientist will tell you," Brad said. Only I could hear him.

Stop being cryptic and tell me what I don't know.

"Have you ever heard the saying if you die in your dreams, you die in real life?"

Sure.

"What if I told you not only is that true, but its truth is mostly down to magic, not science?" Brad looked up at me. "Constance, dreams are their own magical worlds—worlds in which your soul is *supposed* to be the only one to exist."

12

DREAMING 101

By their early forties, most witches knew a lot more about magic than I did. They grew up not only knowing magic exists, but with witch moms who taught them what they knew. Quite often, they had familiars in the family who passed from generation to generation like Twinkie, Trish's mouse familiar who'd belonged to Trish's mother.

Like Trish and Twinkie, my situation with Brad was similar on the face but different. While Brad had been my mother's familiar, he hadn't passed directly to me. There was time where he belonged to no witch—a moment in time where he was free.

It was this moment—and the lies he told me about it—which caused the strife in our already rocky relationship.

So, I'd started my witching journey behind the curve.

My magical learning reminded me a lot of high school. As I learned new things about magic, I was ready to be free of lectures and out in the world doing. Except like in high school, when confronted by the real magical world, it was eye-opening and scary.

It didn't help that Brad fed me information piecemeal.

This new tidbit—the notion that dreams took place in their own world—sent me reeling.

I questioned everything I'd learned so far. Everything about the shadow realm—the world between our world and every other. Then there was magic itself. Who had it and where did it come from?

The little I knew told me witches and wizards were supposed to be the only beings alive with direct access to it.

Back at the sheriff's department, I'd used my access to spell the whole of the building, including Dave and Mac, to forget we were ever there.

The spell was a simple memory charm. It worked on several basic magical principles. It was based on time. There had to be a short duration, not spanning more than minutes or hours. There had to be a need to use it.

At one time, I thought Mom's memory had been taken in a similar fashion. I was wrong. It was too much for such a simple spell.

I'd fill in Dave's gaps later, hoping he could be as lenient with Doug as he was before. Although I didn't think Doug wasn't leaving anytime soon. Just because he dreamed the robbery didn't make him any less guilty in light of the evidence.

The good thing was, he wasn't likely to up and disappear on us. Not easily, anyway.

The bad thing was, I was no closer to figuring out why he dreamed that he robbed the bank. And no closer to figuring out who, if anyone, was behind it.

My only guess was Morgana had something to do with it, not a mystery vampire. It was a guess without any evidence to back it.

Without the gift I'd received from the mother, I was

working on gut instinct alone. My instinct about my gut instinct was to second guess it.

We regrouped at Gran's house. Mom was in the living room watching Mother Gaia knows what. Brad and I took our usual spots in the kitchen. We'd been here many a time, hashing out problems. Me at the table with a steaming cup of coffee. His raccoon-self beside the bowl of cat food.

It was too bad I couldn't see Brad as a Labradoodle puppy. Puppies are much easier to forgive. They can poop all over the house, tear up family heirlooms, and still be fed the next day.

There were two empty places at the table. Two voids in the conversation. Gran's chair was empty. So was the worn silhouette of a cat on the table where Stevie used to let Gran stroke his fur.

I mindlessly drummed my fingers on it.

"You can talk, ya know?" Brad said. "Unless you'd rather I read your mind."

I shook my head. "I don't get it."

"What's not to get?"

"For one—the logistics. How does your soul travel to another world when you're asleep?"

"Think of it like this. Instead of creating a portal through the shadow realm. The shadow realm creates a portal through you. You step through it every night when your conscious self is at rest."

"Okay. Fine. Except mere mortals don't possess magic. How are they doing it?"

"It's not *their* magic," Brad boomed through a mouthful of kibble. "It's the Mother's. Honestly, it's one of Mother Gaia's better ideas."

"Why, though? Why does she really need to trick us into sleep?"

"You realize the world used to be a whole different place, right? Sleep was a scary thing. The body needed it but the mind, well, the mind preferred to stay alive. The Mother gave humans dreams so they might welcome this nighttime ritual. And for the most part, it works."

"Why didn't you tell me about this before?"

"It never came up." Brad shrugged. "And why would it? For the most part, dreams are the kind of magic that you don't need to know about. It's like the magic that put the sun the perfect distance from the Earth. You don't think that was mere happenstance, do you?"

"I don't know what I think."

"You believe in magic. You know it exists. You know the Mother is the life force behind it. If there's a problem with dreams, she'd know about it."

"I see where you're going with this, and I don't like it."

"Just think about it."

I knew Brad wasn't going to pry while I did. I thought until my coffee got cold. I microwaved it and thought some more.

"Still," I said as if the conversation was still going, "none of this explains the disappearances. Like you said, if people die in their dreams, they'd just die."

"Maybe," Brad boomed. "Maybe not. I've never seen it happen. No one has. Not really. It's a theory. And you've seen the *other* side. Are dreams and the afterlife much different?"

"I guess not." I sighed, recalling the brief time spent with my father after his death—the time I took a potion to separate my soul from my body, flew through a portal into the shadow realm, and walked in a world with spirits.

"Are you ready to get a second opinion?" Brad asked. "Someone's been trying to reach you—and not about your car's extended warranty. This someone has firsthand knowledge of walking in worlds she was never meant to be in. She'd know if something is wrong with dreams."

I grumbled. I dragged my feet up the stairs. It amazed me what I was willing to do for answers. Because no matter how mad I was at Brad, it was nothing compared to the hurt —the pain I felt inside—since the day Gran left.

13

MIRROR, MIRROR

Somehow, even when we lived quite literally a world apart, Gran was able to bring out the worst in me. Which was why I hadn't spoken to her in months.

Gran had used her attic as a witching space. Late in the night—the witching hour—I used to hear her heavy footfalls above my head as I tried to sleep in the spare bedroom on the second floor.

The attic was large enough not to be called cozy. Yet it felt small—Gran had managed to fit an oversized cauldron in the middle of the room.

I hadn't touched anything since she left. Her potion ingredients and books were on a bookshelf in the corner of the room. There was a sewing table minus the sewing machine, plus a spinning wheel. And a desk. Gran's things were as untidy as she'd left them.

They were ready for her upon her return.

If she returns.

She'd left a twenty-sided die next to her ruby ring and a necklace I suspected held a decent bit of magic.

Beside them was the object I'd come here for—the mirror.

Mirrors are like portals to other worlds. It made them dangerous. If large enough, they can be used as doors.

After a certain demon had slipped into my head, Gran and I destroyed every mirror in this house. Every mirror save this one.

The mirror was small. I could barely fit my hand to the wrist inside it.

There were probably hundreds of different ways to contact Gran through the mirror. I chose this spell for its potential to grate on her nerves.

"Mirror, mirror, in my hand.
Who's the grouchiest witch in that other land?
Is she mean and does she care?
Can she even hear my prayer?
I call to you, grandmother, not so dear.
If you answer, please don't talk off my ear."

A faint greenish glow came from the mirror. I could no longer see myself or the extra chin, given the angle. There was a blur of green energy, and a distorted image came into focus.

Gran held her own mirror so all I could see were her gray blue eyes and an ample amount of forehead. Just like our video calls when I lived in California.

"It took you long enough to get back to me," Gran spat. "How long has it been since I talked to Brad? An hour? A day? A week?"

"A day... or two," I lied.

"It feels like a week." In the other realm, there was only the concept of time with no construct. Gran adjusted the mirror; now I could see nostrils and lips. "When I call, you should answer. It might be important."

"Or it might be nothing," I said. "Like the last dozen times we talked."

"No. The last dozen times I called, you didn't answer."

I tried to figuratively bite my tongue but couldn't stop myself. "You know, when you left, I thought it meant I wouldn't hear from you so often."

Or at all.

"No," she snapped. "You hoped it meant that."

"Not fair!" I argued. "I'd never say that."

To your face.

"I know you're mad at me. You don't have to deny it."

"I won't," I said.

"Tell me why."

"You know why."

Gran frowned and changed tactics. "How's your mother?"

"Fine." I shrugged. "Mostly the same."

"I wish I could see her." The mirror zoomed out and in as if Gran was trying to get a vantage of everything behind me.

"She's not up here. She doesn't understand what this is."

"She doesn't understand a telephone either, but I'm sure you take calls around her. You should bring her up to the attic. It might help jog a memory."

"The mirror confuses her," I said. "And Brad says she doesn't really have memories. At least none he can see."

"You've told me. I still don't understand how that's even possible. She should have all the memories of her life—at least up until the point she became the bird."

"They aren't there," I said. "Anyway, that's not what I called you about."

"Oh?" Gran's eyes narrowed. "So, you called me, huh? Here, I thought you were calling me back. But that's not something you want to do anymore, is it?"

"Gran," I pleaded. "Can we not?"

She huffed. "Fine. What's going on? How can I help?"

"Really? That easy?"

"One time pass," she said.

"I don't know. Maybe I should save it."

"My girl, what part of *one time* don't you understand?"

"Okay. Okay." I told her about Doug and his dream. Then about the disappearances the vampire had told us about.

Gran's frown deepened with every word I said. She turned away briefly as if to speak to someone else. No words came across, but Gran nodded, then her face filled the mirror again.

"We're not aware of any major issues with dreams or dreaming." Gran's tone had completely changed. It wasn't bitter. If anything, it was soothing, almost as if the mother were speaking through her. "It's not to say there aren't any. Dreams are individual. They can be manipulated by so many outside forces. When taken to the dream world, things like stress or exhaustion or fear can wreak havoc on it."

"When taken to the dream world," I repeated and a thought—a good one. "Can you take something else, something with you to the dream world?"

"It *is* a portal," Gran answered in Mother Gaia's soothing voice.

"So... yes?"

She nodded and the edge of her lips curled in a slight smile.

It was gone in a flash. Gran was herself again.

"There's something else," she said. "You two—you and your mother—are in danger."

"When am I not?" I shrugged a shoulder.

"If you're talking about Morgana, I already know. I kind of figured as much."

"Not Morgana."

"Then who is it?"

"I can't say."

"You can't or you won't?"

"Time is different here. I can't tell you much. Only that you're in danger."

"Is this why you've been calling here? To tell me, but not tell me, about a threat? What are we supposed to do? Sit around and wait for their attack?"

"Of course not. But it's imperative your mother remember who she is. And how she got to be the way she is right now."

"Morgana," I said.

"Not Morgana," Gran reiterated. "Try to include her in your magic. The more she's around it, the more she'll remember."

"I don't need her to remember magic." Gran was frustrating. "I need her to remember being my mother."

"You can't pick and choose what memories she gets back, Constance. I know you don't like hearing it, but magic is the key. Magic can unlock her mind and bring back her memories. You just have to let it. Help her see what she's able to do. Maybe knowing she's able to will help her fight whatever it is stopping her from remembering."

"I'll think about it."

"Do more than think about it. If I was there I'd—"

"Except you're not here," I said, unkindly.

"What's that supposed to mean?"

"It means you up and left us, and I'm here—I've been here—picking up the pieces. You don't get it. That person down there isn't my mother. Not really. Not yet."

"Then help her remember. Show her your magic."

"I can't," I said. "I don't know how to do this without you. I thought we were in this together. We both wanted Mom back. How could you just leave when we finally found her?"

"I don't want to argue with you, but I didn't just up and leave. I gave you hints my time on Earth was coming to an end."

"You mean when you were being cryptic? Which was all the time, by the way. When you said you were leaving, I thought you meant when you died, which I assumed was a long time away."

"Constance."

"What, Gran? What?"

"The truth is I didn't want to get in your way. I had plenty of time with Serena."

"Plenty of time?" I scoffed. "Before she disappeared, you hadn't seen each other in years."

"That's not exactly true," Gran said. "We—I always had a mirror. I had years and years with your mother. I have more fond memories than you have memories with her. I'm sorry for the way things have turned out. And I will be there for you, for her. There's just something important I must do first."

14

IN WITCH TRISH DATES

A week passed without anything too crazy happening. There were no disappearances. No visitors from other realms. No mirror calls from Gran either.

Everything seemed to be in order, which in Creel Creek is never a good sign. Surely, something was waiting around the next bend.

I hoped to get ahead of it—whether it was another disappearance or something else.

Morgana weighed heavily on my mind.

Is she scheming? Surely, she is.

I called a gathering of the local witches. Everything needs a ringleader—its herder of cats. For our monthly coffee chat, it was me. Like a lot of things in the last several months, I'd let it fall off mine and everyone else's radar.

At the bookstore, the crew congregated after what was supposed to be the morning coffee rush. Today, the weather was keeping everyone at home with their coffeemakers.

I'd only served a handful of lattes before Trish arrived.

Even though I saw her almost every day, the truth was,

we rarely spoke about magic. And while I'd seen Kalene and Lauren Whittaker several times in recent months, I was eager to catch up with them outside of the Faction.

The trouble with Lauren was she always brought it up.

"I've never met a real live vampire." She wiped fog from the window with the sleeve of her sweatshirt.

The air conditioning had fogged up the windows, making it nearly impossible to see out.

Outside, it was gray and misty.

Still, Lauren's big blue eyes searched Main Street for Kalene's pickup truck.

"It's not like they're a big deal," Trish said. "We used to work for one. Remember?"

"What was that like?"

"Boring," we said in unison.

Dissatisfied with the window, Lauren eased open the door. "Still no sign of Kalene," she said.

"I doubt she's coming." I finished my latte, frothing the milk and pouring a flower pattern into the espresso. Happy with my work, I sank into one of our cozy cushioned seats.

It was the kind of day I wanted to be at home reading a book.

"She'd be here if she wanted to be." Trish found a stool. "It's not as if she's missing anything except a rainy day."

"She's embarrassed," Lauren said, peeking one last time at the rain. "I feel bad for her."

"Why?" Trish was about as unconcerned for Kalene as a person could be. They weren't enemies, but they weren't exactly friends either.

"You were there," Lauren said. "You saw it. She let a vampire get the best of her."

"Yeah, well, I get why she's embarrassed. I just don't get why you feel bad for her."

"Cause they're friends," I told Trish. "Some friends actually have empathy for each other."

"Right." Trish stretched. "If you're insinuating that's not me, then you're right."

"Oh, I know I'm right. Hence why I said *some* friends."

Merritt, Lauren's daughter, snorted a laugh into her coffee mug. She looked about as un-Lauren-like as was possible. She was tall where Lauren was short. She had blonde hair. Lauren's was black as night with a few flyaway grays.

Those few grays were the only indication Lauren and Merritt weren't the same age. Lauren had been a fully-fledged witch for years. Merritt wouldn't be one for another decade.

"Hey! I might not have much empathy, but I *am* a good friend," Trish argued. "I'm there if you need me. Y'all know that's true."

"Speaking of friends—" Trish eyed us "—I notice Summer Shields didn't get an invite today."

"That was for your benefit," I told her. "I see the looks you give me when her name comes up."

Trish and Summer had a long-standing grudge, dating back from before Summer knew magic. Trish had once hexed Summer bald. The redheaded reporter now wore her hair spiky and short. Despite Trish's hex, it looked cute.

Over the last year, Summer had become a good to friend to me, but she and Trish still had their differences.

Then again, so did Trish and everybody.

"There you go, pointing out another one of my flaws," Trish said. "I don't read between the lines or any of that crap."

"Noted." I chuckled.

Lauren sighed. "I'm afraid Kalene needs us to read

between the lines. We need to get her out of this rut. It's doesn't help that Ivan's leaving in a few days, and she thinks it's her fault."

Here and I thought it was my fault.

"Wait! Ivan's leaving?" Trish arched an eyebrow. "When? Why?"

"You didn't tell her?" Lauren shot me a puzzled look.

I shook my head. "Secrets. Faction. Remember?"

"It's not a Faction secret," she said. "Not when he checks out of his hotel room. The whole town's going to know. The hotel staff treat him like an honored guest."

"As they should," Trish said. "He's basically lived there for what, a year? Almost? He should've got an apartment. He should've got an apartment at my complex—if I referred him, it would've knocked a hundred bucks off my rent."

"Then you would've been neighbors with Ivan." She thought even less of Ivan than she did Kalene.

"I know." She smiled. "That's why I'm lamenting after the fact. I had this idea months ago and kept it to myself for that very reason."

Merritt snorted again.

"Anyway," Lauren cut in, "you should both go to his going away party."

"When is it?" No one had told me about it. I had a sinking feeling I wasn't invited.

"Tonight. At the usual spot."

"Tonight?" I checked the lunar calendar on the wall above the checkout counter. "There's a crescent moon tonight."

Lauren pursed her lips. "So... we'll do both?"

"Maybe." I looked at Trish.

She shook her head. "I'm afraid I can't make it."

"Not to the going away," I said. "But you'll be at the circle, right?"

"The circle?" Trish acted as if she had no clue what I was talking about.

"Crescent moon. Witching hour. Graveyard. This ring any bells?"

"Oh, that?" She screwed up her face. "I guess I forgot to mark my calendar."

"I thought the moon was your calendar. You scoffed when I put that up." I pointed at it.

"Yeah, well, that was before."

"Before?"

"Before I started dating again."

We waited for the punchline. When there was none, Lauren and Merritt squealed. "Good for you."

I was even more confused. "You—you started dating again?"

"You're right," Trish replied. "Again isn't the right word. But yes. I started dating."

"When?" Trish's cheeks reddened, and I grinned.

I was happy for her. So happy. Which I knew she would hate.

"A couple of months ago." She rolled her eyes. "See. This is why I didn't tell you. Look at you three—beaming like idiots all because I said I was going on a date."

"We're not beaming," I said. "We're just happy for you."

"We are," Lauren added. Then she asked, "How long have you been seeing this guy? Does he have a brother or an older widowed father? I'm not picky."

"Neither," Trish said, flustered.

"What about a son?" Merritt asked.

"Afraid not," Trish said flatly. "Y'all are ridiculous. Look at the pair of you. Now, look at me."

"All three of you are perfect." It wasn't what they wanted to hear.

Trish's eyes narrowed. "Don't you even start, Miss Oh My Perfect Boyfriend's Going to Break Up with Me."

Lauren scowled. "She said that?"

Trish nodded. "I told her she was being dumb."

"Don't." I waggled a finger in her direction. "Don't try to turn this around on me. We need details. Who is he? Have you been dating him this whole time? What's his name? Height? What does he do?"

"Again," she said, "why I haven't told you until now. I'm already regretting it. You know what? I should perform a memory charm." She raised her finger.

"Please don't." Mine was raised too.

Lauren held hers at the ready. "I really hate memory charms. I'd rather you not."

"I'd rather escape this conversation." Trish snapped and sent a magical spark our way.

We all ducked.

"Fine. Don't tell us." I winked at Lauren, hoping she'd follow my lead.

"I saw that." Trish's finger stayed leveled at me.

"What?"

"You winked."

"I didn't."

"You did!"

"Why would I wink?" I asked her. "If you don't want to tell us about him, you don't have to."

"You have that look in your eye," Trish said. "It's the look you get when you're working something out. I'm not sure I like it when it involves my love life. Scratch that. I know I don't like it."

"I have no clue what you're talking about," I said.

"I'm just as confused as you," Lauren told Trish.

"Same here," Merritt added.

"You guys are no fun."

"What is it?" Trish asked me. "If I know you, you've already thought of a thousand ways to whittle me down."

"Wrong," I said. "I just thought I'd ask Twinkie when you went out for lunch later. Then I'd call Lauren and give her the details. But no—y'all just couldn't play along."

"I didn't know what I was playing along to." Lauren scrutinized the books behind the counter. "Where is Twinkie?"

At the sound of her name, the little mouse scurried from a stack of books. Her ethereal voice in no way matched the tiny package it came from. "What's up?"

"We were just wondering about Trish's new, uh, significant other."

"He's not significant," Trish said. "And she doesn't know a thing about him."

The little mouse squeaked. "I could know something if I wanted to."

"You wouldn't." Trish was so sure of her and Twinkie's relationship. I wished I had that same security when it came to Brad.

"You're right," Twinkie agreed. "I wouldn't. Sorry, Constance. I guess if you want answers, you'll need to head over to Orange Blossoms tonight around 6:30."

"6:30? Really? If the date's that early, why can't you come to the circle by midnight?"

Trish smiled sheepishly. "Because I'd like to still be on the date—if you know what I mean."

"We know what you mean," Twinkie said. "Also, TMI."

Trish laughed. "TMI for the entity who can literally see into my brain."

"Tell me about it," I grumbled.

"More trouble with Brad?" Twinkie asked.

"No more. No less." I returned my attention to my cup of coffee.

We left it there.

Trish was happier to talk magic for a while. We discussed Doug's dream, swapped a few potions, then speculated on what Gran's important task could be.

Merritt and Lauren left at lunchtime, leaving us stuck in the shop for the next couple of hours without much to do but clean.

The whole town was inside because of the rain. If I wanted, Trish would allow me to leave early. If I kept asking her about her date, she'd insist.

I hated being on her bad side, so I kept quiet. I dusted the shelves and swept the floor. When I put the broom away, Trish relented.

"His name is Scott," she said.

"What?" Who knew keeping my mouth shut for a few minutes would do the trick.

"And no," she said. "I haven't dated him this whole time. I started out using one of those apps. It sucked. But I realized dating's not too hard if you put yourself out there."

"So, you put yourself out there?"

"Not literally. I just made a better profile. I was honest. And Scott digs honest. I like him."

"That's great, Trish. I'm happy for you."

My phone began to ring.

"Who is it?" Trish eyed the screen.

"Just my Perfect Boyfriend." I ran for the back room before Trish could find something to hurl in my direction.

Too late. A spark flew overhead "That's what you get for making me spill my tea, then running off to gush with your boyfriend."

I ducked for cover and answered the phone, laughing.

On the other end of the line, Dave sounded less amused. "I need some help," he said, his tone hushed and breathless.

Before I could ask why, he continued, "He's gone, Constance. Just gone."

"Who is?"

"Doug," Dave answered. "He's—he's disappeared."

15

CREEL CREEK AFTER DARK

EPISODE 140

It's getting late.
Very late.
You hear something go bump in the night.
Are you afraid?
You should be!
Welcome to Creel Creek After Dark: Season Two.

I vana: Well, hello again. It's me, your host, Ivana Steak. With me today is my cohost—

Athena: Athena Hunter.

Ivana: And we're joined by—

Rush: A troublemaker named Rush.

Ivana: Too right, you are, Mister Rush. I have a bone to pick with you. Get this. Today's his last day in studio.

Rush: To be fair, I warned you months ago.

Ivana: You did. Then you stayed and stayed.

Athena: I thought you must've fallen in love.

Ivana: With who? Mister Rush, are you dating?

Athena: I meant with Creel Creek. I'm not sure we ever do it justice on the podcast. You all hear about the weird things going on. You don't see the beauty. You don't know the people like we do. There's a magic here that's not really magic at all.

Ivana: Oh, well, that's true. Mother Earth worked her magic here. That's for sure. Of course, it's not enough for Mister Rush. When are you leaving? And where are you going?

Rush: Soon. And to be honest with you, I don't even know. I'll go wherever the wind takes me.

Athena: In other words, he'll tell us when he gets there.

Ivana: Well, let me be the first to say, your presence here *will* be missed.

Rush: Thanks, Ivana. I appreciate it.

Ivana: Now, on to the topics of today. First up, a bit of carryover from last week. You'll never guess what happened to our bank robber. You remember—the one who claimed it was all a dream.

Athena: As I understand it, he escaped.

Ivana: Athena! Let's not be coy about this. Let the sheriff tell his tall tales. You—and our listeners—know exactly what this means.

Rush: I believe you're insinuating he disappeared.

Ivana: I am. In fact, I'm sure of it.

Athena: Prisoners do escape, Ivana. Not all the time—but it's not exactly uncommon.

Ivana: I'm with you. I even did my research. They escape from the courthouse. From transfers to other facilities. Sometimes, from outside the jail. But this young man escaped from his cell—a cell with no signs of being tampered with. Please, someone, explain to me how that's possible.

Rush: I can't.

Athena: Yeah... neither can I.

16

SUMMONING STEVIE

I t took Dave a few minutes to explain the situation and another minute to tell me how I could help.

Doug had been in his jail cell when it happened. There were no cameras in the cell. No witnesses. And no sign of escape—which thanks to *Shawshank Redemption*, I pictured as a poster of Raquel Welch with a giant hole behind it.

Despite that, they were treating it as an escape. What else could they do? More than half of the inmates at the county jail were regular mortals. So were most of the guards. They wouldn't—they couldn't—understand something like this.

When Dave asked for help, I thought he'd want me to go there and perform a summoning spell—in hopes of finding hidden magical clues inside the cell.

Except that wasn't what Dave was asking for.

No, he had specific questions, and he hoped I could help find the answers. Dave knew enough about the magical world to understand we must be dealing with something from the shadow realm. And it was likely Doug had been taken there, just as Kara Huber had been.

Dave wanted to know where in the shadow realm Doug might've been taken. More than that, he wanted to know if there was any hope of bringing the young man back to our realm in one piece.

I was, of course, at a loss. I hadn't gotten anywhere with Kara Huber's disappearance. How was I supposed to know?

Dave wanted me to ask Brad.

I had a better idea.

———

TYPICALLY, when summoning otherworldly entities from the shadow realm into ours, it was imperative to do things by the book.

There are several steps to get right, else it's possible to set that entity free in our world. I'd dealt with the repercussions of such things—demons and ghouls set loose on our world.

The first step of the process is to snare them in a circle of reinforced magic. Gran had a silver circle embedded in the concrete foundation of her garage. Inside it was a hexagram and an interior pentagram, complete with runes.

Often, she made an exterior circle of salt just in case the interior circle somehow failed.

I didn't have the time or patience to go all the way to Gran's house.

I set up shop in the back room, clearing out space in the center of the dusty floor, which I swept hastily.

There was an old box of chalk deep inside a filing cabinet. I found the least broken piece and drew an elongated circle. Not my best work. I drew a pentagram inside it with a smaller circle at its center for the entity to stand inside.

The second step of summoning is an offering.

I searched for spirits, and luckily, we had some—a half empty bottle of Armand Vineyard's red blend.

Next, I needed to find something cold. We didn't keep ice cream or any good treats in the freezer. The cooler had several gallons of milk. I took one.

I set the wine and the milk on two points of the pentagram, then admired my offering.

Trish scrutinized it from the doorway. "That's got to be the worst summoning circle I've ever seen. And maybe the worst offering in history."

"It's Stevie," I said. "He won't care."

"Oh, he'll care." Twinkie was crouched atop Trish's shoulder. "Remember, he hasn't felt air conditioning in six months. He hasn't felt any human comforts. He's stuck in a wasteland of spirits."

I looked down at my offering and frowned. "No one ever told me it was a wasteland. What should we do?"

Trish rolled her eyes. "Do you always forget you have magic or is it only when you're in a rush?"

"Is that a trick question?" I asked her.

With a wave of her hand, the bottle filled with wine and the milk transformed into a pint of Ben and Jerry's Chunky Monkey.

"A rhetorical question," Trish said. "I know the answer."

I summoned Stevie using a rhyme similar to the spell used to summon his predecessor, Custos the Conniving.

Stevie had taken Custos's place after the demon pleaded with the Mother to allow him reprieve from his realm. With his trickery, Custos had both hindered and helped us get my mother back from Morgana.

Like Brad, Stevie had made his own mistake.

I harbored no ill will toward either of them. I just hoped the same could be said of their feelings for me.

With a puff of black smoke, Stevie manifested inside the circle. He was tall, brawny, and angelic. He looked much like a marble statue come to life. His thick black hair brushed his broad shoulders, which were bare. A sleeveless tunic covered him down to his knees.

His white wings were folded neatly, their torn and broken feathers almost, but not quite, hidden in the folds.

The former familiar turned jailer of spirits looked around the room, and smiled. "I'd say it's a surprise you're the first to summon me, except we both know it's not."

Seeing Stevie's baritone come from lips put me off my game—and I wasn't really on it to begin with. I was so used to his cat form.

It was Stevie's talking cat act that dragged me into this witchy business to begin with.

I searched for a snarky reply. Gran would've found one. I didn't. "It's good to see you, too," I said.

"What's with all this?" He picked up the wine and studied the label.

"Offerings," I said.

"Is that ice cream?"

"Chunky Monkey."

"Huh." He nodded happily. "Maybe I should get summoned more often. You know I could break this circle in about a second, right?"

"You wouldn't though," I said.

"You're right. I wouldn't. But just so we're clear, it's not because I owe you or anything. We aren't family, Constance. Not anymore. You understand that, right?"

I found my snark. "I get it," I said. "I really do. But I want you to understand something. I know why you won't break the circle. It's because it's too easy. You're stubborn, just like Gran. You chose to take Custos's place.

"No matter how awful it is there, you'll stick around until the job's done. You won't take the easy way out."

"Your confidence amuses me." Stevie put the wine down at his feet. "I like it. It's something you've always needed more of."

He rose to his feet. "Is that Trish and Twinkie hiding behind the door? Long time, no see."

"We're just here for moral support," Trish said.

"She doesn't need it," Stevie boomed. "Didn't you hear me? She needs confidence. She needs to fight her own battles, summon her own demons and the like."

"Are you a demon now?" Twinkie asked.

"You know what I mean." Stevie skirted the question. "Go ahead, Constance. Ask your questions. I'll allow you two free of charge."

"Why haven't you taken the offerings?" I asked him.

"I'm counting that as one," he said. "And I'm not taking your offerings because I don't want to. I'm not a demon. Nor am I some shadow world fiend. But there are rules I have to abide by. I want to help you. I really do. So, make your next question good or else I'll leave here and we'll both be disappointed."

Stevie meant the rules of summoning. It was a give and a take, even if he wasn't accepting the offering of wine and ice cream.

I had to condense several questions into one. "Okay," I sighed. "Where else, besides your realm, can someone be trapped?"

"What a vague question." I started to defend it but Stevie held up a finger. "Don't get me wrong. I like it. It should allow us to get the details you need. Who's trapped and are they a witch, a wizard, or a shifter?"

"A young man named Doug," I said. "As far as I know, he's a regular mortal."

"Of course he is." Stevie clicked his teeth together, thinking. "I'll tell you in the short period of time I've been over this realm, I've taken in six prisoners and freed eleven. None of the six were regular humans. In fact, only two were mortals."

"You've freed eleven?"

"No more questions," Stevie said. "And they're nothing to worry about. It was the end of their sentence. They were returned to their respective realms where they still reside. I put a trace spell on all of them. You can never be too careful.

"Now, let's get back to the question at hand. Where else can someone be trapped. Only the guardian or the owner of a realm may grant entry. You might not remember it, but you met a guardian when you visited your father on the other side."

I remembered.

"The same rules apply to the exit. What I'm saying is almost any realm could be used as a prison."

"Great. That narrows it down then." Trish's words dripped with sarcasm.

"This line of thinking won't get us anywhere," Twinkie said. "What we should be asking ourselves is how. How does someone get taken from our world to this other realm? Did they go through the shadow realm? Through a portal? There's only so many of those."

"He couldn't have used a portal," I said.

"Why not?"

"Because there's no portal where this person was."

"That's good," Stevie said.

"Why is it good?" Trish asked.

"I thought you were for narrowing down possibilities," Stevie said. "We've narrowed it down to every other way to another world."

I knew I wasn't going to like the answer, but I asked the question anyway. "How many of those are there?"

"Several billion," Stevie said. "All of them as unlikely as the next. At least we're on the right track. If I can get a picture of what happened, maybe I'll think of something. What were the circumstances? Don't spare a detail."

I told him about Kara Huber, and how she winked into nothingness. Then I told him about Doug, his mysterious bank robbery dream, and his disappearance. "Dave says he's vanished," I said. "Just like Kara."

"Did someone—anyone—see it happen?" Stevie asked.

I shook my head. "No one saw it. He was in a jail cell. Alone."

My heart hurt for Doug. He'd been so hollow. So out of it.

I hung my head, frustrated our conversation had gotten us nowhere.

A black Doc Martin scuffed the outer chalk ring. With it, the magic of the circle was snuffed out.

A moment like this could mean one of two things. The entity could be freed into our world. Or a powerful witch could send the entity back from which it came.

Trish was a powerful witch.

Stevie disappeared—just like Kara and Doug.

"What'd you do that for?" I was shocked by Trish's actions.

"A couple of reasons," she said. "We don't need him anymore, and he was letting this Chunky Monkey go to waste." She picked up the ice cream and the plastic spoon I'd set beside it. "Look. It's melted."

"I like it a little melty," I said.

"Me too." She dove in while I searched for an extra spoon.

I thought surely she was going to explain, instead she savored every bite of ice cream.

I stole a bite. "Stevie's going to be pissed."

"Bah. He'll get over it. Twinkie can fill him in next time they talk."

"Speaking of, are you going to tell me why we don't need Stevie anymore or am I supposed to guess?"

"I had a thought." Trish spooned another mouthful. "You said Doug was alone. I'm not sure that's true. See, Doug might've been the only *person* in the cell, but there's actually a chance—a solid chance—he was there with a ghost."

17

LURQUE RECHARGED

"Everyone knows about the ghosts at the Creel Creek Mountain Lodge," Trish said.

"Not there anymore. Remember? They left."

We'd closed the shop early and were driving out of town in Trish's yellow bug. It was still dreary. The gray sky converged with the gray hills to make a normally serene landscape a blotchy mess of abstract art.

Sheets of rain splattered the windshield. Trish drove without caution, tires spinning through every curve in the road.

"Yeah, well, the legend of the ghost will never die," she said. "Anyway, let's just say the lodge and the vineyard aren't the only places around here with ghosts. I told you about my dad, right? How he killed my mother and took her powers."

"How could I forget?" When she'd told me, it had somehow solidified our friendship. We both had tragedies in our past. We'd both lost our mothers and our fathers.

"It might surprise you, but I spoke to my father a few times after everything went down. Weirdly, it was how I processed the whole thing. He was in jail at the time, awaiting trial. One thing that sticks out is him telling me how active the ghosts were in there. Like I cared."

"Wait. He was in jail? How'd that work?"

When she'd told me about it, she said because of Willow's vision, Dave saved her life. I assumed he'd saved hers by taking another.

I hadn't pried any further. Those weren't the type of conversations I liked to have. Not with Dave. Not with Trish.

"Your Gran actually spelled his cell," Trish said. "He couldn't do magic inside it. He could still sense it though. I was getting closer to forty, and my powers were starting to show. I swear he wanted me to come see him on the off chance I or someone else let their guard down."

"Trish, I'm so sorry."

"No. It's fine. Really. By now, I'm used to my personal traumas helping you out of a pinch. Just don't be surprised when I cash all this goodwill in."

She swerved off the road and up the winding path to Armand Vineyard. In true Trish style, she opted to hex its gate open rather than roll her window down and fiddle with the buzzer.

I gave her a look.

"What? I didn't *need* to get wet."

I couldn't blame her. The rain was really coming down.

At the top of the hill against the backdrop of gray sky, the house looked more like the Addams Family house than usual. The house was complete with a butler who reminded me of Uncle Fester.

Lurque opened the door but failed to greet us. He walked past us out into the rain. He gazed skyward like a child seeing snow for the first time. "I love the rain," he said.

Thunder rumbled, shaking the earth below our feet.

"And I love the thunder," he said. "But it's the lightning that sustains me."

Lurque's bald head was slick with rain. The dark bags under his eyes made him look like he hadn't slept in decades. He sighed with contentment, then went back to the door.

"Hello, ladies," he said as if he hadn't already spoken to us.

"Hi, Lurque." I smiled. "Is Cyrus available?"

I didn't feel right asking for Mr. Caulfield. Him being a ghost made things weird. The owner of the vineyard, Cyrus, was his own brand of undead—Osiris, the supposed Egyptian god of the afterlife. Or at least, Cyrus was the basis for the concept of said god.

"Is this a social visit?" Lurque asked. "We do prefer you call ahead a week in advance for any social calls."

Cyrus traipsed down the stairs behind the butler. As usual, he was dressed to the nines in a linen suit with shined shoes and a checkered tie.

"When is it ever a social call with these two?" he asked.

Lurque contemplated the question. "There was the one time."

"No, Lurque. I believe you're mistaken," Cyrus said. "If you recall, even that dinner had some business there at the end."

The butler shook his head and under the collar of his shirt, I saw the bolts attaching it to his neck. "Too right, sir. Shall I send them away?"

"If it were so easy." Cyrus laughed. "Please set out some tea and biscuits, I'll escort them to the dining room myself."

"Very well, sir." Lurque bowed. A burst of lightning lit up the front steps and Lurque jolted upward. He marched away with pep in his proverbial step.

"This way, ladies." Cyrus ushered us in the other direction. "I was just finishing up a tasting. I'm sure you won't mind helping me finish the bottle. After all, I assume I'll be assisting you with something in the hereafter."

"Actually," I said, "we kind of need Mr. Caulfield's help."

"You need Eric, huh?" He turned, leading us into a stately office. On a large mahogany desk, there was a bottle of wine and a tall, almost full glass. Otherwise, the desk held an open notebook and a pen.

A bluish orb of energy burst into the room from the opposite wall. "I heard my name."

The ghost had once been the manager of the grocery store and a vampire. While he resembled his fleshy self in many ways, the outline of his features blurred into nothingness. When he moved too fast, I could barely tell he was there at all.

"They need your expertise," Cyrus said.

"What is it?" Mr. Caulfield asked. "What's the monster of the month this time? A vampire?"

"Not a vampire," I said. "I don't think."

He shook his ghostly head. "Ghosts don't interact with the living world. Not directly. Whatever you're looking for, it can't be a ghost."

"It's not a ghost we're looking for," Trish replied. "It's ghostly information."

She explained why we came. Then Mr. Caulfield went looking for a ghost who might've seen what happened.

Cyrus led us to the dining room, and we ate and drank for about an hour, waiting while the storm raged outside.

Flashes of blue lightning illuminated the closed shades. Each time, I was sure it was Mr. Caulfield returning.

When we were done eating, Lurque barged into the

room. He threw the doors open almost as if he didn't know his own strength. The bags under his eyes were gone.

When he tried to take Trish's plate, it flew nearly to the ceiling. He caught it with ease, then did the same with the others, as if it were a parlor trick.

"I told you it would be a good storm," Cyrus said.

"A great storm," Lurque replied. He bustled out of the room with a smile.

Not a minute later, Mr. Caulfield returned with another ghost. A man. Short in stature. His features were just as undefined. There was a nose and a mouth, eyes, and what might qualify as ears.

I didn't recognize him, but Trish seemed to.

Her mouth fell open. "Dad?"

18

A GHOSTLY RETURN

A t first, I didn't understand. After our talk in the car, I assumed Trish's father went from jail to prison, and she never saw him again.

If Dave hadn't killed him then how did he die?

Why is he a ghost? How is he ghost?

With ghosts, the rules were up in the air, so to speak. I knew the basics. They had to die in some tragic event. Even then, they might still accept their death and move on. It took a stubborn spirit not to.

Given his relationship to Trish, I assumed Mr. Harris erred on the other side of stubborn.

The room had gone eerily quiet. Cyrus's face contorted into a look of both shock and horror.

Ghosts are already pale but somehow, Mr. Caulfield managed to punctuate the rule. His ghostly form brushed against a bookcase and half of him disappeared into it.

Trish's father did quite the opposite. He puffed out his ghostly chest with pride. "My girl. My beautiful girl. How wonderful it is to see you after all these years."

"I can't say the same." Trish's voice quivered. Her snarky confidence was gone.

"I, uh, I didn't know who he was," Mr. Caulfield said. "Else I never would've brought him here. Trish, I'm so sorry. We can send him away."

Mr. Caulfield had been alive—or undead—when Trish's mother was killed. He knew the story better than I did.

Trish shook her head. "If he has the information we need, then he can stay—at least until we get it out of him."

"You do realize I'm right here in front of you?"

"Oh, we know," I said. "We just don't care."

"I don't believe we've had the pleasure." Mr. Harris's voice was slick and sweet like a car salesman's.

I hate car salesmen.

"Don't you worry about her, Dad."

"I can't be happy you finally have a friend? And another witch. How interesting."

"It's not," Trish snapped. "If it wasn't for you, I would've had plenty of friends in school. You're the reason I never wanted to bring anyone over."

"You can only blame me for so much."

Cyrus stepped between them. "I'm not one to interfere in a family squabble but I believe we've wasted enough time already."

"Right." Trish took a deep breath, collecting herself. "Daddy," she said slowly, "tell us about the man who disappeared, then get out of here while you still can."

"Is that a threat, my girl?"

"You bet your specter ass it's a threat. I'm serious. I'll send you to where you're supposed to be."

His chest deflated. "I'll tell you what I know, but only if you do something for me in return."

"Never," Trish said.

"That wasn't our deal," Mr. Caulfield said.

"Deals change," the ghost said flatly.

He *was* a car salesman.

I could see this wasn't going anywhere. And I could only be a fly on the wall for so long.

I already regretted what I was about to say. "I will. I'll do it—that is, if it's a reasonable request."

"So reasonable," he said. "Barely an inconvenience."

"What do you want?" I asked.

"No, no." He put out his arm, which faded into nothingness well before a hand and fingertips should. "First, I'll tell you what you want to know."

"Fair enough."

Trish's nostrils flared. "He doesn't play fair, Constance. Whatever he wants, he thinks you're going to give it to him."

"She will." He sounded confident. "Now, about this young man who disappeared. What do you want to know?"

"Everything," I said.

"Then I'll tell you everything." Mr. Harris inflated his spirit body again. He bobbed above the dining table as if he wasn't already the center of our attention.

"The young man you're referring to came into the cell— my old cell—about a week ago. He didn't eat that night. He didn't talk, aside from a curse or two. He stayed awake until the wee hours of the morning, then dozed a little. When he awoke, he wasn't happy. I don't know why. Later in the afternoon, they took him for questioning. Then they brought him back."

"Seriously?" Trish let out a big sigh.

"What? She said she wanted to know everything."

"Maybe get a little closer to the event?"

"Very well," he deflated. "I didn't think much of it at first. Jail is hard on everyone. But the boy didn't sleep the next few nights. Not a wink. Every time he caught himself about to doze off, he got scared. He'd fill the sink with water and splash his face. A couple of times, he even dunked his whole head in it. He'd be wide awake again for an hour or so, then he'd have to start over. This might be important."

"You're probably right," I said.

"Course I'm right." Mr. Harris rose higher in the air. "Anyway, it went on like this for days until finally, one night, he looked out our window—if you can call it that—and he begged the sun not to go down.

"As you can imagine, it didn't oblige.

"I felt bad for the boy. He was a tormented soul. He reminded me of me."

"Save it," Trish sneered. "What happened next?"

"That night, he finally succumbed to sleep. I'll tell you, it wasn't a restful sleep either. He tossed and turned, and the next morning, he wasn't at all himself. He spoke more in the next hour than he had since he got there."

"What did he say?" I asked.

"Well, at first, I thought he was talking to me. It was a one-sided conversation, almost like someone else was in the room. Someone I couldn't see."

"Was there someone?"

"I don't think so. He was talking nonsense, mostly. But I do remember his last words. He said, 'You're right. I guess I'll go with you.'"

"And?" I was at the edge of my seat, even though I already knew the outcome.

"Then he wasn't there anymore."

Mr. Harris circled the room and came down for a landing near my seat. "There," he said. "I held up my end of the bargain. It's time for you to hold up yours, Constance the Witch."

"Don't call her that." Trish rolled her eyes. Growing up with a father like him, I couldn't blame her for developing the habit.

"What is it?" I asked. "What do you want?"

"I can sense your magic," he said. "You're Jez's grand-daughter, aren't you?"

I nodded.

"There's something she kept hidden all these years. Something I've heard quite a lot about since becoming a ghost." His ghostly face grew grim. "The magical mine," he said. "I'd like to know its location. It's *precise* location."

I don't know what I expected, but that wasn't it. I hadn't thought about the mine since it nearly collapsed on me and Summer Shields. We barely escaped with our lives.

As far as I knew, its magic was no longer accessible to the outside world. It was no longer something my family had to protect. The duty had been passed down by one of Creel Creek's founders from generation to generation, ulti-mately to Gran, then to me.

"What do you want at the mine?" I asked him. "Ghosts can't interact with the living world."

Cyrus cleared his throat. "There's an exception to the rule."

I had a sinking feeling in the pit of my stomach. "Let me guess. Magic?"

The silence of the room confirmed my suspicion.

I didn't know what to do. What to say. I couldn't give Trish's father magic. It was what got him in trouble in the first place.

"Well," he said eagerly, "where is it?"

Usually, I didn't mind bending magical laws. I'd allowed a demon an hour in our world. I'd promised a little girl she could be a witch when she was supposed to be a werewolf.

This was different.

I wasn't used to going back on my word. But in this case, I did.

"I can't tell you," I said.

"You can't or you won't?"

"Won't." I smiled.

"Witch," he barked. "I can make your life a living hell. You've heard of hauntings on TV, but you've never experienced their truth. The spirits I'll drum up will give your nightmares nightmares."

I expected some backup. For Trish to say something snarky. For Cyrus or Mr. Caulfield to come to my defense.

They didn't say a word.

I shook my head in disgust. "You aren't getting what you want. Not today. Not ever."

"You don't understand who you're up against. I'll haunt your loved ones."

I thought of Mom. She was likely still in bed, sleeping to the music of rain on the roof.

The hairs on my neck stood on end as magic rushed to my fingertips. I was angry.

"I think I'll take my chances," I said.

"Look at me," the ghost demanded. "Look at what I was willing to do—to sacrifice—for the things I want. You don't have the guts or gumption."

"Dad," Trish said. "You don't know her."

"Tell me I'm wrong then."

"Just go," she pleaded. "She's not giving you what you want."

He ignored her. "I'll give you one last chance to come to your senses. Tell me where the mine is."

"I'm sorry," I said.

"You're sorry?" He laughed. "You sound like the judge when he sentenced me to the chair."

My question about how he became a ghost was answered. The words slipped out of my mouth. "So *that's* how you died."

It was the wrong thing to say.

Trish's eyes went wide with surprise. At the same time, the ghost's smile broadened, as if he'd sprung a trap. Only I wasn't the prey.

I was the bait.

"My girl hasn't told you then." His blue eyes brightened as they flitted over Trish, who was silent and still. "It wasn't the chair that got me. It was her. She cursed me to die."

Whether it was a lie or the truth didn't matter much to me. Either way, it was the last straw. I was tired of Mr. Harris —of his manipulation and threats.

I wasn't holding back any longer. I let it go.

Without even a spell, the magic came out in a quick burst of golden energy. It arced above the table and landed in his midsection. The magic swirled in his ghostly belly, and he made a face like he was going to be sick.

Then the ghost of Trish's father exploded into a thousand tiny pieces of pale blue light.

19

IN WITCH MOM TAGS ALONG

"**F**igures he's going to put it like that." Trish didn't stop to check if the highway was clear; she went full throttle down the drive and out.

We left hastily and without a single protest from Cyrus or Mr. Caulfield, who seemed happy to see us go.

It didn't matter. There was plenty for us to unpack ourselves.

"I didn't curse him," she said. "I came into my powers, and I took my mom's back—which I had every right to do. How was I supposed to know he'd bound his own lifeforce to them?"

"Why do that?"

"To make himself more powerful—obviously. There's just the small catch that if you lose said powers, you also lose your life. Mom used to say he was overly ambitious. He had the drive without the means. I think she was putting it politely."

"He was kind of a jerk," I said. "Still, he gave me an idea."

"Yeah?"

"Nightmares," I said. "When I was talking to Gran the

other day, Mother Gaia told me we bring things with us into our dream world. Things like stress. And nightmares are the result. What if Doug brought something else into his dream world?"

"Like?"

I shrugged. "Something."

"I'm glad Dad could help. It was kind of a shock, seeing him. I didn't know he was a ghost."

"I know," I said. "He's not really gone, is he?"

In my gut, I knew my magic hadn't done permanent damage. I just had to hear Trish confirm it.

"I don't think so," she said. "He'll probably be back. The good thing is, whatever that spell was back there, it scared him. He won't make good on those threats. Not for a while."

"Good." For a second, I was relieved.

"Seriously though, what are you going to do if he does haunt you? What if he haunts your mom? Or the girls?"

My relief was short lived.

"What am *I* going to do?" I scoffed. "He's *your* dad. Didn't you say something about banishing him to where he's supposed to go?"

"I was totally bluffing," Trish said. "That's powerful magic. Mother Gaia level magic. Good thing you have an in with her."

"Sure. I'll ask her for another favor. I'm sure she won't mind."

"You know I can tell when you're being sarcastic."

"It's kind of the point," I said. "I can tell when you are, too. It's when your mouth opens and closes."

"Hardy har." She stopped behind Prongs in the parking lot, giving me a short sprint in the rain.

The sky was still full of dark clouds. Neither the sun, nor the crescent moon, were in sight.

"You have a plan for tonight?" she asked.

"I don't know. What I do every crescent moon?"

"Try to take over the world?"

"Nope." I shouldered open the door. "I wing it and hope for the best."

———————

WHEN I GOT in the car, I called Dave, explaining what we'd learned about Doug's final moments and about my nightmare theory.

Unfortunately, this information was of no use to him. Because of the odd mix of paranormal to regular mortals, his office had to treat the disappearance like an escape. There were deputies at checkpoints along the highway, searching railcars, and everywhere else across the county.

They had to go through the motions like it was any other case. And, of course, Dave would be working late.

I offered to pick the girls up from their after-school activities.

I fed them. They bathed. We read some books. And somehow, through no fault of my own, I missed Ivan's going away party.

Shucks.

Dave got in close to midnight, leaving me little time to get to Gran's house and prepare for the witching hour.

I hurried inside, hoping I'd find Mom ready to go. I found her watching TV and eating a bowl of dry cereal.

"Seriously, Brad? You couldn't set out some clothes for her? Help her find the milk?"

"She drank the last of the milk yesterday. I would've sent you a mental note, except I'm not allowed in your head."

"When it's about Mom, you're allowed."

The raccoon clambered onto the kitchen table. "And as for the state of her, you said you didn't want to take her out tonight. With today's rain, I thought you might cancel as well."

"Fair enough," I said. "Let's get her ready and go."

Brad nudged a book on the table. "This might help."

It was the family grimoire Gran had given to me. I'd already combed through it several times. "There's nothing worthwhile in it," I said. "I've checked."

"It's not for a spell." Brad shook his head. "It's for her. It's something she used to see growing up. Maybe if she holds it when y'all go up the hill today, it'll jog something loose."

"Good idea." I had to give it to Brad, he was trying— which was more than I could say for myself.

I'd shut him out for so long now. The truth was, sometime in the last few months, I'd forgiven him. And I never stopped doling out punishments.

"You want to know what happened today?" I asked him.

"Of course," he said. "Tell me."

I shook my head. "You're welcome to look."

I couldn't feel when he was in my head; only in this moment, I knew he was.

Mom got dressed, and we trudged through the damp woods behind Gran's. The path was littered with wet leaves. I avoided the giant puddles. In her rubber boots, Mom splashed in them like a child.

The witching hour was nearly over when we made it to the clearing. On cue, the clouds parted and a small sliver of moon shone down on an old oak tree at the top of a hill.

Brad stood guard outside the graveyard's iron gate. Inside, we climbed the slippery grass of the hill.

Just as I had the first time I'd brought her here, I showed

Mom what to do. I put my palm on the tree's trunk. It glowed with traces of magic.

She mimicked me. The outline of her own hand was pale blue light. Her magic.

Our magic intertwined, gold and blue, racing up the bark of the tree and changing the colors of the leaves and the moss. The tree lit up like a beacon on the hill.

This had happened before. When it had, I was sure it meant something—that she'd have her memories. Her voice.

No such luck.

I stood beneath the beauty of the tree, and I was jaded. It wasn't anything spectacular. It wasn't a magical mystery. It was a magical chore. An effort I was sure would result in nothing, much like Dave's search for an inmate who disappeared into another world.

I rattled off a few spells. Some from memory. Others, I just made up.

From time to time, Mom would smile, encouraging me. In her other hand, she held the grimoire. It, too, took on the hue of our magic.

"What am I not seeing?" I asked.

No one was there listening. Not Gran. Not Mother Gaia.

"If only this tree could speak," I said.

Mom shrugged.

After a while, I gave up. Another failure.

We walked home, hand in hand. Mom's way of reassuring me I'd done nothing wrong.

Except, obviously, I had.

I was ready to throw a pity party for one. I even had a plan. While Mom watched TV, I'd open a bottle of wine and sink into the tub to wash off the dirt and the grime from this walk in the woods.

"You know," Brad interrupted my thoughts. "Parties are better with a crowd."

"You're not invited." I jogged up the steps of the back porch, shook out my rain jacket, and eased open the back door.

"What about them? Are they invited?"

At first, I didn't get his joke. But Brad's comedic timing was impeccable.

Sitting at the kitchen table—and already drinking my bottle of wine—were Summer Shields and Lauren Whittaker.

20

A CARDINAL CLUE

M om didn't seem to notice the two extra women in the kitchen. Or if she did, she didn't care. She fixed a cup of coffee and zipped out to the living room without even acknowledging them.

If only it were that easy for me.

"Be nice," Brad said.

Lauren's big blue eyes were glazed over, moving aimlessly from me, to Brad, then the refrigerator.

I waved my hand in front of her face and she startled. "Oh, hey, Constance."

"What are you two doing here?" I took the seat between them—Gran's old chair.

"We were trying to make the circle," Lauren said dreamily.

"Yeah, the circle." Summer was worse off, barely able to keep her eyes open.

How they'd managed to open the wine was beyond me. Then I took a closer look and realized it wasn't my wine but a cheap bottle from who knows where.

"Well, ladies, you're late," I said. "It wasn't much of a circle tonight anyway. Just me and Mom."

"Sorry," Summer slurred. "We got lost."

"Y'all didn't—you didn't drive here, did you?"

"We're not stupid." She pointed at the corner by the garage door. A standard broom and a tattered industrial mop leaned against the wall.

"Not stupid?" I laughed. "Could've fooled me. Seriously? You thought flying was safer than calling an Uber?"

"Creel Creek doesn't have Uber," Summer said. "We have that other one though."

"You know what I mean."

"From the looks of them," Brad said, "they should've got a room at the Inn."

"I'm not disagreeing with you. But they're here now." I took their bottle and sniffed. It smelled okay. Like wine.

It was time to play catch up. I drank it straight from the bottle, then shuddered as it hit my tastebuds. "Why doesn't the lodge carry good wine?"

I got up and went to the liquor cabinet—otherwise known as the cabinet above the fridge. When I was a little girl, Mom used to hide candy and other treats in the same location—a habit she'd picked up from Gran.

I dug out an old bottle I'd taken from the vineyard on a previous trip, grumbling because our quick exit meant I'd failed to replenish our store.

"I think you mean why don't they carry Armand Vineyard wine?" Summer asked.

"Sure." I uncorked the wine.

"It probably has something to do with the feud."

"Feud? What feud?" Lauren wasn't really paying attention. She was nodding off, only catching every other sentence or so.

"Between the owners—the Osmonds—and Cyrus." Summer waved off my offer to refill her glass.

I poured my own. "How long has it been going on?"

"I don't know. About sixty years? They've been in this feud about as long as the Inn's been open."

"So, they know about Cyrus?"

"Well, no, they believe it's a family feud. It's something to do with the ghosts, I think."

After I covered the news of my encounters with Cyrus and a ghost, we got to talking about the *other* news of the day—Doug's disappearance.

We being me and Summer. Lauren had fallen asleep with her head cocked at an awkward angle. She was going to hurt in the morning.

Summer had sobered a little as I went the other direction. "So, you think nightmares are to blame?"

Lauren jerked and nearly fell out of her chair. "Nightmare?" She yawned. "I wasn't having a nightmare, was I?"

"You weren't," I said. "And you can go lay down on the couch if you want."

"No. I'm awake." She yawned. "Go on. What about nightmares?"

"Nightmares happen when you bring something into your dream world. Something like stress or exhaustion. Or maybe someone."

"Like?" Summer scowled.

"I don't know, but I'm leaning toward Morgana. Think about it. We know familiars can do things like this. She took over my mom's whole body. Maybe now she's taking over dream worlds."

"It's possible." Brad made his way into the conversation. "It would explain why I haven't been able to find her in the shadow realm."

"Exactly—because she's not using it. She's using dreams to move through realms."

"It still doesn't explain the disappearances," Brad said. "Where would she take these people and why?"

"I didn't say I'd worked it all out."

"There's a delicate balance here," Brad said. "If she were to harm these people—or worse, kill them, then the Morgana we met would no longer exist."

"I'm not following."

"She'd become a demon," Lauren said.

Lauren knew more about demons than I did. She'd dealt with one living inside her head for a while. The same demon had only a brief stint in mine.

"Maybe it's not her," she went on. "Maybe it's a demon."

"No." I shook my head. I was adamant—I was sure I was right about this. Then again, my gut feelings weren't what they used to be. "I mean. Maybe."

"I'm with her," Brad said. "This is two different problems. You're trying to combine them into one."

"Okay, so maybe it's a demon." I thought about it—about each disappearance. "Except—how's the demon getting in? They aren't looking into mirrors before they disappear. They're looking up in the sky."

"It could be a bird," Lauren suggested.

"A bird?" Summer made a face. "If that's true then I'm in big trouble."

"Why?"

"I swear there's this bird hanging around everywhere I go."

"What kind of bird?" I asked.

"A cardinal."

I was reminded of Mom. When she was the owl, she followed me across the state.

"Morgana," Brad boomed. "She's traded places with someone."

"You think she did it again? So soon?"

"Why not? That's her modus operandi. Not dreams."

"You'd have to see the bird to prove it though. And we still wouldn't know who it is, would we?"

"I think I might know." Summer leaned forward. "It's Jade. It's got to be. Why else would this bird follow me? And I told you, she hasn't been herself."

"How so?" Lauren was fully awake or trying to be. She paced back and forth in the kitchen.

"Did either of you listen to the podcast today?"

We both nodded.

"Right, so we recorded it just after I did my story about the escape. Dave had asked me to leave out a few details, and I did. I didn't tell Jade there weren't any signs of escape."

"Then how did she know?" Lauren asked.

"She's a familiar," I said. "She read her mind."

Summer turned to Brad, who had curled up on a cat bed on the floor. "Speaking of, if it's really been Jade this whole time, how come you didn't figure it out? Wasn't that your main job the last few months?"

"I was searching the shadow realm for signs of her," Brad said. "As a person, she's nearly impossible to track."

"Why?"

"I need to see into your eyes to see into your mind. In your everyday life, how often do you come face to face with a raccoon?"

"Not very," she admitted. "Do you think she—Morgana —knows what it is we're up against? Do you think she has a grasp of this, this demon?"

"She might," I said. "It also fits her M.O."

"Great." Lauren grimaced. "We're going to have to fight again."

"What's the plan?" Summer asked.

It took a minute to realize they were both looking at me as if I knew what to do.

The wine had gone to my head—even thinking about trivial things felt like hard work, let alone this.

It had taken almost a year to plan and coordinate the effort to let Custos out in our realm for a mere hour. Even then, it all went to hell. Both literally and figuratively.

He did hand us Morgana on a plate, Brad reminded me. I wasn't sure if I liked him being in my head again, but now wasn't the time to kick him out.

"Hmm." I concentrated and it made my head hurt. "First thing in the morning, Brad needs to confirm the cardinal isn't actually a cardinal, that it has some semblance of humanity inside it."

The raccoon nodded.

I focused on his eyes, which glowed with reflected light. "Then," I said, "if you're up for it, find Custos and maybe he can help us narrow down what demons have connections with nightmares. He owes us at that much." I turned to Summer and Lauren. "Finally, I guess we'll have to confront Jade."

"It's not going to be a simple confrontation," Brad said. "You'll need to trap and bind her."

"You mean, we'll have to trick her into walking into a circle." It wasn't going to be easy.

Summer frowned. "Shouldn't Brad verify it's her, first? You know. Just in case I'm wrong."

"You're right," I said. "I can feel it. Plus, if she sees Brad, she'll know we know. She might run."

"Or fight," Lauren added.

"Good point," I said.

Now, fully invested in the conversation, Brad clambered up onto the table, ensuring he had our attention.

"Do understand, she's in control of Jade's body. Even though *it* might not have out-and-out magic, that doesn't mean she won't. She's aware of the stones. She might have held a couple in reserve. If we're going to do this, we'll have to plan it out with care and precision."

"What do you mean *if* we're going to?" Summer asked.

"Let me put this delicately." Brad showed his teeth in what could only be described as a wince, his eyes on the living room where Mom was captivated by the television. "We don't want to repeat past mistakes. If we do this wrong, Morgana will just hop to the next body. And there's no guarantee Jade will ever be her true self again. At least while Morgana's here in Creel Creek, she's contained."

"What about the demon?" Lauren asked.

"Brad will talk to Custos. We'll take it from there."

"It's not much of a plan," Summer said.

"It's not," I agreed. "Maybe let me sleep on it? Y'all stay here tonight. No more drinking and flying."

In my head, Brad spoke to me and me alone. *I know it feels like a leap to trust me with this,* he said. *Thank you.*

Don't thank me yet, I thought. *Most of this lands on your shoulders.*

I'm aware. He climbed down from the table, snuggling into the cat bed again.

Do you think we stand a chance of getting this right?

Against one or both? he asked.

Your pick.

We take them down one at a time. I can't be in two places at once.

I'm not asking you to be. I knew I was asking a lot of him, but in my head, I was focused on Morgana. He could deal with the demon.

Constance, he thought, *I know you'll fight me on this, but you'll need my help with Morgana.* I hated how Brad could read my mind—even the parts I didn't want him to see. His beady black eyes bored into mine. *And yes, I know she's the priority.*

21

IN WITCH I AIN'T MISSING HIM
AT ALL

The next morning, I woke up with a hangover. Lauren had passed out in Gran's old bed. I let her sleep.

I went downstairs.

Mom was still awake, helping Summer make breakfast in the kitchen. The smell of bacon and eggs wafted through the house. More importantly, so did the aroma of coffee.

I poured a cup and hunkered down at the table.

I noticed Brad's food dish was empty and so was the cat bed. "Where's Brad?"

"He didn't want to wake you." Summer spooned eggs onto a plate. "It was simple, really. All I had to do was go outside. The cardinal fluttered down to the porch railing."

"And?"

"It's just as we thought," Summer said. "Brad's headed to the shadow realm now to search for Custos. He said not to do anything until he returns. None of us should be around Jade—not without sunglasses."

"Crap." My coffee was without its usual splash of milk. "I guess I'll have to run to the convenience store."

There'd be no grocery runs until the Morgana situation was figured out.

"No need." Summer opened the fridge. She handed me a carton of milk. "I used magic."

"Now, that's convenient." Magic responds to need, and now we had reason *not* to go to the grocery store.

After breakfast, I dropped Lauren and Summer back at their vehicles, still parked in the lodge's parking lot. So was Ivan's nondescript Caprice Classic.

"I guess he hasn't made his exit yet," I pointed out.

"Tomorrow," Summer said. "You'd know that if you went to the party last night."

I channeled Trish and rolled my eyes. "Should I say bye?"

"I wouldn't. Or rather, I'm not." Summer made a beeline for her car.

Lauren did the same. She smiled and waved, getting into her own Subaru.

The thought lingered. I wanted to feel bad for *not* wanting to tell him goodbye. But I didn't.

Eventually, I was going to have to tell him about Jade and the demon. It didn't have to be today. Part of me reasoned that if I told Ivan and he went to see Jade on his way out of town, then it was me putting him in danger.

Except Ivan wore sunglasses almost everywhere—a part of his incognito style.

I knew Ivan's room number but shuddered at the thought of being alone with him. Our last conversation weighed heavily on my mind.

After easing into an open parking spot, I shot him a text asking if he could meet in the lobby.

It was empty this time of day. No one checking in or out.

The front desk clerk was on break. There was a sign saying to ring the bell for service.

I waited in the open space by the unlit fireplace. Like the rest of the inn, it was reminiscent of an old cabin with wooden floors and trophy heads on display. There were several deer, a moose, and a full-sized bear in the corner of the room. Four oversized lounge chairs on a cowhide rug were arranged parallel to the fireplace.

I sat down and watched the lone elevator only to be surprised by Ivan coming from the other direction.

"Constance," he said. "This is a surprise."

Tell me about it.

"Oh, well, I was in the neighborhood."

"You missed quite the party last night." He rubbed his throat. "My voice is hoarse from the karaoke. My wayward son carried on too much last night—if you know what I mean."

I feigned a laugh. "Yeah, sorry I missed it. That's why I'm here. I wanted to say goodbye. I didn't know when we'd see each other again."

"Not for a while, I'm afraid." He took the chair across from me. I thought his face looked calculating.

It was an expression I knew too well. I'd seen it in the business world on clients and even colleagues—as if we weren't friends, but rivals.

Then it was gone, replaced by a warm smile. "How are you holding up?" he asked. "Quite the development in the case you're working. Another disappearance. But like I told you before, don't be surprised when the trail runs cold."

"I think it's a demon," I said.

"Oh?"

"It waits until they're in their dream world to take over their mind. It's genius, really. Instead of them being behind the wheel but unable to drive, they're almost completely oblivious to the fact it's there."

Since talking it through with Summer and Lauren—and sleeping several hours—our theory had solidified into something more coherent.

"It's good." Ivan nodded. "Maybe even spot on. Still doesn't explain how they disappear. Or why."

"I know. I'm working on it."

"How exactly?"

"Brad," I told him. "He's going to find out about demons for me." For whatever reason, I didn't want to reveal my source in Custos and left that part vague. But I did have another thought. "Speaking of familiars, where's Vertigo? I haven't seen her."

"Oh." He kind of shrugged. "She's around here some-where. You know, for some reason they don't allow birds in the building."

"Right." I chuckled, thinking of the time thousands of birds aided in our escape from the lodge's convention center.

We wouldn't have been trapped there if it wasn't for Jade.

I knew this next part would be hard for him to hear. "There's something else I should tell you," I said.

He cut me off. "Did you consider my question? Will you be my eyes and ears while I'm away?"

"I, uh—"

"It's all right. Let's sort it out. It's not a big deal. I'm sorry for how I came across the other night."

He was coming across just as persistent now, reminding me even more of Halitosis Hal. The truth was I had thought it over, and it still felt like a trick.

It frustrated me because in our time together, Ivan hadn't made many missteps. He'd come through for me—

for the Faction—more than once. The glaring omission on this list was the night against the ghouls and Morgana.

"What was that the other night?" I asked him.

"Mostly, it was stress." He reclined, interlacing his fingers, and put his head against the headrest of the large chair. He crossed his feet at the ankles. "Everything with Kalene got to me. I made a mistake sending her there."

"Why did you send her to the vampires?"

A smile crossed Ivan's face when the front desk clerk came over. She was tall, thin, and tattooed with a big stud in her nose. Her hair was all the colors of the rainbow.

Either Ivan was genuinely happy to see her or he was relieved not to answer my question.

"Mister Rush," she said. "I'm so sad to hear you're leaving us. If there's anything you need today, I'm happy to assist."

"Oh, no, I'm fine. Thanks, Yanni."

"You're welcome." She flashed him a smile. Her face soured as she gave me a once over before returning to the desk.

"She's going to make a great witch one day," Ivan said. "I hope we see her name in here." Ivan kept the register, his little black book, close at hand. "You know this is the reason I've got to go. I wish I could delegate these duties."

"Why can't you?"

"I just can't. Besides, I like doing it. Listen, Constance, I'm sorry, but I must insist you do this for me. There's no one else I can trust with it."

"Trust," I said. "It's a big word."

He frowned. "What is it? What do you need to tell me?"

I relented. "It's about Morgana. We think we've found her."

"Really?" He wasn't fazed in the slightest.

I shook my head and barreled through the explanation. "Don't you get it? It's Jade. She's in Jade. And she's been under our noses the whole time."

"Well, that's not exactly accurate." The smile stayed plastered on his face. "She hasn't been under my nose. No—she's been under my thumb."

"What?" I couldn't believe what I was hearing. "What do you mean? You knew this whole time and you didn't tell me?"

"It was for your own good."

"How and how?" Pure anger bubbled inside me like lava about to blow.

"How did I know?" he asked, amused. "See, Constance, I knew because I'm the one who put her there."

22

IN DREAMS

After hearing a myriad of excuses—none of which I cared to believe—I left the Creel Creek Mountain Lodge unsure if I ever wanted to hear from Ivan Rush again.

One thing was sure—I wasn't going to be his quote-unquote eyes and ears while he was away.

I spent the rest of my day off at Dave's house. Knowing the search efforts were moot, he volunteered himself to work the late shift.

We ate lunch together, watched a movie with the girls, and played a handful of board games before the girls got good and bored with our company. The littles went to Allie's room to watch her play a video game. How watching someone else play constituted entertainment boggled my mind, but they seemed to enjoy it.

I cuddled up with Dave on the couch and he threw on some mindless TV—a cooking competition. It was then I realized there wasn't much difference between watching people cook and watching someone else play a video game.

We'd already gone over everything—from the disappearance of Doug to Morgana taking Jade's place and Ivan's role in it.

It had taken Dave a long time—even longer than it had for me—to get comfortable with Ivan. Now our loyalty to him had come to an end.

"How could he do this and not tell you?" Dave's voice rumbled against my ear on his chest. "I know she was responsible for you being put up on stage at After Dark Con. Put in that trance. But this isn't an eye for an eye. What if what he's done does permanent damage to Jade?"

"I'm afraid it might."

"If so, he'll have to own it. That's his burden to carry for the rest of his life. Is he going to help change her back? Get rid of Morgana?"

"Nope. He said I'll figure it out. Eventually."

"What's he expect to happen when he goes away?"

I sighed. "He thinks she'll continue to behave until I find a better solution."

"What do you think?"

"I think it's not fair. I never liked Jade, but she doesn't deserve this. It's Morgana who deserves to serve time for what she's done."

"I've got an idea," Dave said. "Although I'm not sure you'll like it. I'm not even sure I like it."

"It's got to be better than what I've come up with."

"I find that hard to believe."

"Don't. Cause I haven't come up with anything."

"I find that harder to believe." His gaze was kind and thoughtful. Even though we hadn't come up with a solution, talking it over with him helped slow down my runaway thoughts.

"My mother used to say witches are always scheming," he said. "Of course, now I know she was being as prejudiced as my father. But still, she wasn't entirely wrong. I swear, in times like this, you always seem to have a plan."

"Not this time."

"Granted, I don't always like those plans. It'd be nice for you to stay out of the fire for a change."

"Too late," I said. "But for now, I'm waiting on Brad to get back with news. Or rather, I'm using that as an excuse not to tax my brain. I don't want to do anything without him here to help."

"What about your mom?" Dave asked. "What's she doing tonight if Brad's gone?"

"I asked Summer to check in on her."

"Good." He smiled. "So, you want to hear my crazy idea or what?"

"Do I actually have a choice?"

"Not while I have you trapped." He wrapped his arms around me. "Hear me out. What if Jade broke a law? Heck, she doesn't have to break a law. I could bring her in as a suspect and hold her for twenty-four hours."

"What good would that do?"

"It'd give you twenty-four hours to plan."

"No." I shook my head. "She'd be on to us. She'd know we were planning something. Right now, she thinks Ivan's the only one who knows about their deal."

"What's stopping him from revealing said knowledge if he sees her today?"

"I removed his memories."

"Oh." He nodded. "Huh. You think that's what happened to your mom?"

"No. The memory charm works for a few minutes, an hour tops. It's not going to erase a memory like that. Plus, you have to have a need to do it. Whatever happened to

Mom, it was some sort of magic more powerful. I just wish I knew what."

Dave's arms tighten around me. "I'm proud of you, Constance. What you did today took guts and some magical know-how. Your Gran would be proud."

"Oh, I'm sure she'd find some reason to criticize me."

I angled for a kiss, and he met me halfway. Our lips touched for a mere second when someone cried on the stairs above us.

"Gross!" Allie said. "Get a room."

Dave sighed. "I should probably get ready for work. You're sure you don't want me to make any arrests tonight?"

"Positive." I gave him another kiss.

"Gross!"

———

As the afternoon faded into night, I had other feelings. It wasn't the first time I'd been home alone with Dave's girls with threats looming on the horizon.

But never had there been so many beings wanting to cause us harm.

A paranormal hunter had tried to break down the door, but he couldn't get past the house's wards.

Would Morgana have the same trouble? Would a ghost and his ghostly minions? Surely not. I had a sneaking suspicion either could get past the house's defenses.

Then there was this demon—a demon I knew nothing about. I wondered if it knew anything about me.

Dave's house had a few mirrors. It wouldn't take much for a demon to find its way inside, not the house, but a mind.

"Not good," I muttered to myself.

I put blankets and sheets over every mirror I could find. The downstairs looked worse than the last time Elsie and Kacie asked Dave to build a blanket fort.

Upstairs was no better. I blocked the bathroom mirrors above the sink, and just in case, I spelled the reflective glass of the shower into a swirly gray fog.

Still, I couldn't get to sleep in Dave's empty bed.

How could Morgana be right here in town? How could Ivan think it was a good idea?

The more I thought about it, the more sinister it became.

A crazy thought—crazier than Dave's idea—crossed my mind. What if they were working together? What if Ivan knew Morgana? How? I didn't know. Nor did it make sense. Ivan was in the Faction. And Morgana had all but revealed her hand.

What else could they be after?

More magic?

Or were they the threat Gran warned me about?

"I'm being paranoid," I said aloud. "Ivan isn't plotting against me."

Suddenly, my gut instinct kicked back in. Or it seemed to. Telling me I was wrong. Very wrong.

I didn't have time to mull it over. A small voice wailed down the hall. I ran to Kacie and Elsie's room.

The smallest, Kacie, was tossing and turning in her sleep. I put a reassuring hand to her forehead. "It's all right. I'm here."

Her eyelids fluttered. "I had a nightmare."

"I know."

"Constance," she whispered, "will you stay here in case I have another?"

"Sure."

She gave me about a foot and half of mattress. She sprawled across the rest of the bed.

"Promise you'll stay?"

"Promise." She was so small and afraid. I remembered what it was like when I was alone in my room at night. My dad's room felt like it was a million miles away. "Don't you worry, sweetheart. I'm here for you. I'll protect you."

And I would protect her—whether it was a ghost, a demon, a wizard, or just a regular ole nightmare.

Kacie closed her eyes.

So did I, and I drifted off into a dream.

I WAS RUNNING through a dense forest on a pitch black night. I tripped and fell but didn't feel hurt—just an urge to keep running. So, I did.

My vision became clearer, and I saw a little girl running ahead of me. She had on a long pink nightgown. It floated behind her.

Her feet were bare. No obstacle on the ground fazed her, whether it was a pine cone or a rock.

"Wait up!" I called.

She turned abruptly, surprised to find me there. "Constance?"

"I'm here." Weirdly, I wasn't out of breath. "Where are we?"

I didn't recognize anything about the woods. We weren't near Dave's house or the graveyard.

The little girl shrugged. "It always looks like this. I don't like it. It's dark."

I tried to think back to where we'd been before we got to the woods. I couldn't, and it was frustrating.

I knew where we were. I just couldn't say it. It was on the tip of my tongue.

I remembered tucking Kacie in after a nightmare. It finally clicked.

"I don't like the dark either." I felt a tingle of magic sizzle down my spine, through my arms, and to my fingertips. Something heavy weighed down my hand.

"Kacie," I said, "what don't you like about the dark?"

"I can't see."

"Right." I clicked on the flashlight. "You have one too."

She smiled with delight as her own flashlight lit the path ahead of us.

"How's that?" I asked her.

"It's a little better. I'm glad you're here."

"Where to now?"

She shrugged again.

Kids.

"It's your dream," I said. "Where do you want to go? Where do you usually go?"

"There's a carnival," she said. "But I don't like the clowns."

"No clowns."

"Allie and Elsie make me ride the tall rides. I don't like that either. Daddy says I'm not good with heights."

"No tall rides," I said. "What do you like at the carnival?"

"Prizes!" She ran ahead. "Help me win some prizes!"

The path wove around to the shore of some ocean or bay. Up ahead of us, a pier jutted out into the placid water. The telltale lights of a carnival lit up the horizon, complete with a Ferris wheel, a Tilt-A-Whirl, and numerous other attractions.

"I should never have introduced you to *Big*." I jogged behind her to the pier.

We were the only two people. The games seemed to run themselves. In no time, we'd shot water pistols to blow up balloons, thrown darts, and even tried to make a basket on what had to be the world's tallest basketball hoop.

I had a stuffed tiger, and Kacie held a giant teddy bear. We walked beside the pier's railing looking at the carnival lights reflecting on the water. Small waves lapped against the pilings.

It was as peaceful as a dream could be.

I wasn't even sure I'd done anything to help. I handed her a flashlight. She did the rest, winning us the prizes.

If I'd dreamed a carnival as a kid, it wouldn't have been anything like hers. I loved rides—the taller the better. And as a kid, I had an iron stomach. I could eat a funnel cake and a hot dog, wash it down with soda, then step in line for the Wipeout.

Kacie tugged at my arm. "I don't want to do the tall rides."

"I know." I nodded. "We don't have to."

The dream shifted, so subtle I barely noticed. Kacie tugging at my arm reversed, and now I was pulling her.

But where?

"I don't want to," she cried.

I tried to stop but my legs kept going. We moved down the pier toward a ticket taker for the Ferris wheel. There was no line, just a young man in an white uniform.

He reminded me of Doug—if Doug didn't have tattoos.

The ticket taker smiled and held open his palm. "Ten tickets, please."

"Where'd you come from?" I asked.

"Ten tickets," he said again.

"We don't have tickets. She doesn't want to go." Even as I was saying it, my hand was reaching into my pocket. It came out with plenty of tickets. Enough to ride the Ferris wheel a hundred times or more.

"I don't want to go."

"Kacie!" I cried. "Stop this."

The little girl began to sob. "I'm not good with heights."

"I know you're not. We don't have to go." I dragged her toward the rickety swinging cart.

"Have fun!" The ticket taker held the lap bar open with one hand. It was rusted. He shoved the little girl inside with the other.

"Stop this!" I screamed.

"She can't stop it," the ticket taker said. "It's your fault."

He was right. It was just as Mother Gaia had explained. I'd come here to help but it was my foreign fears causing this nightmare. I'd infused my own troubles into Kacie's dream, and I'd ruined it.

Can I also fix it?

I called upon magic. It tingled in my hands, which were gripping the rusty lap bar. The ride changed, turning into a roller coaster except its track went in an oval with no hills or dips.

It was the perfect ride for Kacie, who wasn't good with heights but loved a good thrill. She squealed with delight as we went around and around.

I learned an important lesson about dreams. The next time I found myself in someone else's dream world, if ever, I was going to let them take the lead.

23

IN WHICH I OFFER TO HELP

W hen I checked on her the next morning, Mom was asleep. Without Brad there to tell me, I wasn't sure if she'd just gone to bed or if she'd been there most of the night.

Summer had popped in around midnight. She texted me saying all was well.

It didn't feel that way. There was an ominous cloud hovering inside my mind. I checked and found nothing out of place.

Still, something wasn't right.

The creepy crawly sensation followed me in to work my ever so vital shift at Bewitched Books. Vital because Trish wanted her beauty sleep.

Usually, I didn't mind working the shift alone. Today was different.

A few minutes after opening the store, I found myself eyeing the window, hoping for someone to come in early. Anyone.

I wanted to shake this odd feeling.

I tried to focus on other things. I organized the shelves—

what we had left. Most of the old bookshelves were gone as we'd reduced our stock of romance, science fiction, and mystery for the profitable side of the business—the coffee bar.

I made myself some of the magical elixir and drank it while checking off the online orders. The shop did most of its occult and paranormal sales through the online store. There were a few on display in a locked case of spellbooks and grimoires against the back wall.

For our not-so-paranormal customers, Trish had spelled the case to look like a display of old magazines. She'd adjusted the spell after a customer asked about buying the lot of Home and Garden magazines.

Now, the glamour played off the customer's likes and dislikes. It looked different to every customer. Betty Everage liked to ask when we were going to throw out the Golf Digest. Autumn Smith turned her nose up at Outside.

Most customers never gave it a second look.

Most.

The first customer was an outlier, spending several minutes perusing what to her looked like old magazines. Her being there did nothing to relieve my nerves. She was adding to them. Something about her troubled me.

She circled the store, looking both dazed and confused.

It's early. She probably hasn't had her coffee yet.

I hoped she'd order one. I tried to get her attention, but she wouldn't meet my gaze.

"Good morning!" My voice sounded so loud in the quiet shop. "Can I help you with anything?"

She didn't seem to hear me.

"Hello? Can I help you?" I asked again.

The woman blinked a few times, but still didn't seem to notice me. She reminded me of Mom—how she silently went about her day without acknowledging much of anything or anyone.

I moved closer—close enough to hear her breathing, which sounded shallow. She stared down. I followed her eyes to the spellbooks.

Could she see them?

Reaching out with my magic, I couldn't sense a magical bone in her body. So, there was no telling what magazines she saw in their place.

The woman was average height. She had shoulder-length brown hair with a few flyaways. She wore business casual—khakis and a blue polo with a bank logo embroidered on the chest.

The same bank that was robbed while I was in DC with Trish.

Does she work there?

Being taller than most women, I tried not to loom or hover over anyone. This time, I made an exception. I scooted closer and waved my hand. I thought I might startle her, but no dice. She didn't move or say a thing.

Maybe I'd been asking her the wrong question.

"I'm Constance," I told her. "Are you okay? Do you need anything? I'm here to help."

Maybe she couldn't hear me at all.

Her head jerked. Hard yellow eyes shot toward the front window. And it was me who was startled. I jumped nearly a foot in the air.

I recovered to find her looking down at me. Her eyes weren't yellow. They were brown. There was nothing outside the window either, just a few birds flying away from the street lamps.

Sunlight glinted off the woman's necklace. She might

not have magic, but the stone she wore—it had once been a powerful source, although its glow had faded.

"Were you offering to help me just now?" she asked.

"I can try."

She nodded but struggled to get the words out. "I believe I—" She grimaced. "I believe I may have killed someone."

24

A DEATH IN THE FACTION

Twinkie was apparently keeping an eye on things.

Constance, her voice came crisp and clear in my head, *I believe a demon was here, in the store.*

Are they gone?

They are now, Twinkie said.

If I looked at the window, at just the right angle, there was a reflection—almost like a mirror.

Is that how the demon escaped? Did it jump into another realm?

I don't know.

To the woman, it looked like I wasn't responding—like I hadn't registered what she'd said. Quite the turnaround from before.

"Did you hear me?" she asked.

I nodded slowly. "I did. What makes you think you killed someone?"

"A feeling," she said.

"Let's take a step back." Ever since she'd confessed to killing someone, I'd wanted to call Dave. To get help. But I knew *she* hadn't killed someone. It was the demon, using her

—maybe even using the magical stone on her necklace. "What do you mean, a feeling? Can you tell me what happened?"

"It's—it's like a dream," she said. "It's like the memory of a dream. Except I don't remember dreaming it. Have you ever heard of something like that? What am I saying? Of course you haven't. No one has."

"You'd be surprised," I told her.

"Honestly, I don't even know where I am. Is this the bookstore on Main?"

I nodded again.

"I've always wanted to try the coffee here." She sighed. "Maybe I'm just being silly. It was just a dream. I don't know what I was saying. I should—I should call my doctor. That's sensible, right?"

There was no telling what had really happened, and it seemed her memory of it was fading fast.

"No, well, yeah, that's sensible. But I'd like to hear about the dream."

"Oh, right, the dream." She struggled. "I, um, I killed someone in it. Can you believe it?"

"Maybe it was just an accident? Maybe they're still alive and we can get them some help."

"It was no accident," she said. "That I'm sure of. I murdered him in cold blood. There was a knife."

I tried to think of everything Dave might ask her. "Can you tell me who you killed—where—and when this happened?"

She frowned. "I told you. It was just a dream. Silly. I haven't been sleeping well. I don't even remember going to sleep last night—let alone driving here. I didn't mean to be here. I think I'd like to leave now."

"Please, don't go." I couldn't allow her to leave. "I can

help you. I can. But I need you to tell me who it was and where they are now."

She shook her head. "I'm not sure of his name. I really should go now."

"Dreams can be so vivid," I said. "I had a dream once that I won the lottery. I woke up, and for a couple of minutes, I was sure it really happened. It took me a few minutes to remember I hardly ever buy lottery tickets."

"Except that's not like my dream, is it? I'm sorry, but I'm not comfortable here. I don't even know you. What's your name?"

"Constance. And yours?"

"Evelyn," she said. "Evelyn James. I'm sorry for giving you a scare this morning."

"That's okay. I'm sorry you had a scare this morning."

To her, it was a dream, and for her sake, I hoped it stayed buried. But it *had* happened. A demon had used Evelyn to kill someone.

The gravity of the situation wasn't lost on me. I had to get answers somehow. I had to call Dave.

I wish she'd tell me where, I thought.

Beside the register, something rustled.

"I really should go now." Evelyn backed toward the door. She hadn't noticed the mouse perched on a stack of books and staring at her.

The mouse waited until she was gone. "I saw it pretty clearly. You're not going to believe it."

"What? Where did it happen?"

"It's Ivan," she said. "He's at the Creel Creek Mountain Lodge. And he's dead."

A TIRED DAVE picked me up a few minutes later. He was supposed to be asleep, and he looked it. His uniform was crumpled as if he'd taken it straight from the hamper and put it back on. I was certain he had.

He gulped down coffee and asked me to explain, for the second time, what this was all about.

"You aren't going to arrest her, are you?"

"Not at the moment," Dave said. "The good thing is, she didn't come to me confessing her crimes. We don't even know if it's true."

"Don't we though?" I asked.

"Twinkie saw a dream. A memory of a dream. If it's like you say, if a demon was there, they could be fooling you. Maybe they're sending you out on some goose chase while they do something else. You locked the store, right?"

"Of course." I wanted so much for the dream to be a fabrication—some scheme of Morgana or the demon. I could deal with a trick. An illusion. What my mind couldn't reconcile was the alternative.

"You really think it's a trick?" I asked Dave.

"I don't know what to believe." Dave blinked for far longer than any driver should. "I guess what I'm struggling with is how Ivan—a powerful wizard—could be killed by some ordinary woman."

"She wasn't ordinary at the time. She was this demon, and she had a stone from the mine."

Dave grunted. "However it shakes out, we need to find this demon. And soon."

"Yeah, well, I've been trying."

"Constance," he squeezed my hand, "I said *we* for a reason. Promise me you won't go at this alone."

The worry was evident in his tired eyes as he drove with lights but no siren, speeding to the edge of town. The blue beams bounced off the lodge's sign at the road. How many times had I been here recently? The last time, I was so mad at Ivan. So angry.

In my chest, there was a hollow where my heart had once been. By the time we reached the lobby, I was completely numb. In a state of shock I'd only known once— when I learned of my father's death.

It wasn't that Ivan and I were close. We weren't.

It wasn't that I loved him. As of yesterday, I didn't even consider him a friend.

We weren't kindred in any way. We shared two things. Magic and the Faction.

Dave and I didn't announce our presence to anyone. There was no staff in sight. We went up to the second floor.

We were careful not to touch anything. Nothing looked amiss. There wasn't a speck of blood or anything outside room 211.

I spelled the lock while Dave put on gloves.

He reached for the doorknob, then gave me a measured look. "You're sure you want to do this? You can always wait outside. Or downstairs. You don't have to see it."

"I have to know if it's real," I said.

He nodded solemnly and pushed the door open.

It was like a horror movie come to life. Some sort of ritual had taken place in Ivan's room.

The curtains hung, not from the window, but from the ceiling like a canopy. There were markings on the walls— runes in a language I didn't know. On the floor, a circle. A perfect circle made of a red substance I could only assume was blood. Ivan's body was in the middle.

The wizard was dead.

CREEL CREEK AFTER DARK

EPISODE 141

Welcome to Creel Creek After Dark: Season Two.

Athena: There are no words.

   Ivana: None.

   Athena: Dear, dear, listeners. I regret to inform you Mister Rush—Ivan—passed away last night.

   Ivana: Please, just bear with us. This is sure to be a heavy episode.

   Athena: We considered canceling this week. And maybe the next week too. We even considered going on hiatus.

   Ivana: Except that didn't seem fair to you fans.

   Athena: Plus, we know the world we live in today. The internet is both a blessing and a curse.

   Ivana: Mostly a curse.

   Athena: The truth is, we wanted to get out ahead of the news. All it takes is one internet sleuth to put two and two together, and the rumors will spread like wildfire.

   Ivana: So, here we are, telling you—the fans—Ivan Rush was murdered.

EYES AND EARS

The rest of the day was a whirlwind. Dave went to work on basically no sleep. I stayed with him as long as I could. He wanted to ensure the scene was authentic—that it wasn't staged and it really was Ivan's body on the makeshift altar.

He had Mac drop me off at Gran's house, and I saw to Mom before Trish picked me up that afternoon.

I wasn't up for driving. My hands were shaky. I couldn't get the picture of Ivan in the middle of that bloody circle out of my head.

Worse than the gruesome display, I had come face to face with the demon. At the shop, I'd seen its yellow eyes leaving Evelyn James. As demons do, it used her for something awful.

I'd done nothing to stop it, and pretty soon, it was sure to do something worse.

I answered a dozen texts and several phone calls. No one wanted to believe it was true. Not even Trish.

"You're sure it was him?" she asked.

"I'm sure."

Trish and I were on the way to Kalene's farm, meeting Lauren and Summer there. Lauren wanted to show a united front, expecting Kalene to take the news of Ivan's death especially hard.

"It could've been a glamour on someone else," Trish said. "Maybe not even someone else. Maybe *something* else."

"Like?"

"I don't know. A pig?" She stared out at the fields. "The whole saying about lipstick on a pig fails when magic's involved. You very much can dress up a pig with magic. I've seen it done."

"It was Ivan. I'm sure of it."

"You know I never trusted him, right?"

I wanted to laugh. Trish's feelings about Ivan were well known, but mine, well, I'd kept them mostly to myself. I hadn't told Trish about my last conversation with him. Or about Morgana taking Jade's body—and Ivan's role in it.

"I wasn't his biggest fan either. Not lately."

"This is so fishy." Trish pulled into Kalene's driveway. "Part of me wants to think Ivan's pulling a stunt. Another part of me believes it's Morgana. He actually said she was under his control?"

"No. I believe the exact words were under his thumb."

"Wow!" Her eyes went wide. "A bold statement coming from the likes of him. It's funny—I never sensed a lot of power when I was around him."

I hadn't given it much thought before, but now I did. She was right. Ivan wasn't the most powerful wizard.

Magic is easy to sense. It's like a breeze. I could sense the magic around us. Trish was high up on the magical spectrum, buzzing with energy. Lauren was in the middle. Summer and Kalene didn't have a lot of magic.

The town was filled with people across the spectrum.

Dave, as a werewolf, had magic, but its only outlet was to shift into the wolf.

There were others who carried around magic without any ability to tap into it. Then there were people like Doug, who'd been under a spell once. They carried residual magic.

We got out of the car and walked to the main house. It was a small cottage, especially compared to the rest of the property. Kalene's farm was a good fifty acres outside of town. She had a barn with horses. Cattle roamed a pasture behind it. There was a pond at the back of the farm with a creek running into it.

Here, I couldn't help but be reminded of my and Ivan's early encounters. I'd introduced him to Kalene. She'd joined the Faction immediately. This was pretty soon after she helped overcome Beruth, the demon who her mother had kept at bay for years and years.

"There's another alternative," I told Trish. "The demon might be working alone."

She shrugged and knocked on the door. Kalene answered. Her eyes were red from recent tears. Her hair was down, not in its normal braid.

"Y'all come in," she said. "I'm sorry the place is a mess. I haven't felt much like cleaning since..." She didn't finish, but we knew what she meant.

Kalene had been hiding since the incident with the vampire. Lauren had made it her personal mission to get Kalene out of her slump, then this happened.

I wrapped Kalene in a fierce hug. Fierce in return—she nearly popped my back.

"I'm sorry, Kalene," I said.

"He was one of the good guys."

I struggled for a response. Trish fell into a coughing fit. I glared at her, and she mouthed *sorry*.

For us, the jury was still out whether Ivan was a good guy, a bad guy, or like most people, somewhere in between.

Still, I wasn't willing to put the blame on him. Not for his own death. Not until we had some answers.

"You need some water?" Summer leaped up from the couch and went to the kitchen.

"I'll be fine." Trish waved her off.

Lauren shot me a tightlipped smile. Her big blue eyes said everything. She was hurting as much as Kalene.

Despite Trish's protest, Summer presented Trish a glass of water, then returned to the couch and offered a question to the room. "So, what are we supposed to do now?"

"Well—"

Kalene cut me off. "I plan to help with his estate," she said. "Not that he has much of an estate. It's just the car really."

"What about his relatives?" Summer asked.

"Ivan didn't have any family. The Faction was everything to him."

"You're sure you can handle it?" Lauren asked her.

"I know a good lawyer who can help me out."

"No," Lauren said. "I mean are you up for it?"

"I knew what you meant." Kalene fought back tears. "I want to. In fact, he wanted me to help. He came by here just yesterday and asked if I could be his eyes and ears while he's away. Obviously, I said yes."

Obviously.

Ivan had a backup plan. Even now, after everything, I couldn't help but wonder exactly what being his eyes and ears entailed. Was it an expression or was it a spell?

I wasn't sure if there was any way to find out. I'd be asking Trish on the way home. If she didn't know, I'd ask Brad then Gran, in that order.

Kalene wiped a tear from her cheek. "Oh, and I was thinking we should do something. A celebration of life. Like a wake. Details to come."

Lauren and Summer nodded.

Trish hadn't paid much attention to Kalene. She said, "What were you going to say, Constance? What's your plan?"

"I'm still waiting for Brad to get back. But," I turned to Summer, "Dave has a lot on his plate right now. He might need your help covering up the gory details this morning."

"No problem there. I'm happy to."

Trish laughed. "You realize a year ago, this would have already blown up in our faces, right?"

"It still might," Summer said. "As soon as the news broke, Jade called me about doing a podcast."

"Wait!" Trish scowled. "Jade? You mean to tell us you saw Morgana today? How's that not headline news?"

"I had to," Summer said. "It'd look mighty suspicious if I was a no show. It's fine though, I wore sunglasses. I told her I'd been crying, which was the truth."

"Same here." Lauren sniffled.

I felt like they were judging me. I had a good reason for not crying. I just wasn't sure about sharing it with them. Not yet.

Then there was Morgana. I hated the waiting game. I wanted to see her myself. I wanted to confront her.

Not only was Morgana the reason my mom was gone for basically my entire life, she was also the reason she was in her current state.

I sighed. "You don't think Morgana suspects we know anything, do you?"

"Hard to say," Summer said. "She's not the Jade I once knew. I mean she's not Jade. She's much harder to read."

"How did she take the news about Ivan?" Trish asked.

"Not great."

"No." Trish shook her head. "What I'm asking is do you think she played a part in it?"

Summer considered. "Again, it's hard to say—she's so guarded. I don't know if I'd call what I saw this afternoon a surprise. If anything, I think she was intrigued."

The conversation gave me goosebumps. If Morgana had planned Ivan's demise, it meant any one of us could be next —with the betting odds on me. "What do you mean? How was she intrigued?"

"I don't know." Summer shrugged. "She wanted me to take the sunglasses off. She asked about the lights in the room like ten times. The good news is, I don't think it had anything to do with suspicion. No, she was out for details."

"Like the details of the disappearance?" I asked.

"Yeah. Like that. But I was thinking—I've been sitting there beside her for months. She's probably been in my head the whole time."

"Is that a problem?" Lauren asked.

"I think so," Summer said, and she looked at me as if I knew what she was talking about.

Trish arched an eyebrow.

I was lost. "What?"

"The mine," Summer said. "I know where it was. I was with you when it collapsed. If I remember correctly, she was after it the whole time she was your mother."

"Right." I felt stupid and small.

"It's collapsed," Trish said. "The magic is buried under tons of rock."

"You really think some rocks are going to stop Morgana?" Summer asked. "What if Ivan was the only thing standing in her way? And now he's gone."

The room went silent. Kalene stood up from the couch.

With her fist clenched at her side and determination written on her face, she said, "Then I guess it's up to us. We're going to stand in her way."

27

IN WITCH I MAKE A DEAL

Trish turned the engine over. "I thought you said the demon might be working alone."

She backed out of the driveway with barely a glance over her shoulder. Being a vigilant witch, Trish had ripped her rearview mirror out.

No demons would find her here. Not unless they had other means of traversing the Earth.

I shrugged. "And I agree with my earlier self. It might be."

Trish kept her eyes on the road ahead. It was her tone that scrutinized me. "Yeah, but you made quite a case against Morgana back there."

"No," I protested. "Summer made a case. After you posed a question." I sighed. "What does it matter? Either way, Morgana's a problem we'll have to face eventually."

The sooner, the better.

"I guess you're right," Trish said. "She is a problem."

A weight had lifted off my shoulders at their resolve to help with Morgana. Not that I was planning to fight her alone. I always assumed I'd have some help. But with Ivan gone and the Faction fractured, I could only enlist those within my circle of trust—a circle that had grown smaller over the last few months.

I trusted Trish and Lauren, and even Summer. Kalene was the outlier. I knew she meant well, but what did it mean, her being Ivan's eyes and ears? For now, I was leaving her out of any planning. That was, once I got to planning.

Between us three witches, we had more than enough power to conquer any single foe. The problem was there were at least two at large.

And that was without factoring in Trish's ghostly father. She hadn't mentioned him since the vineyard.

She fiddled with the radio, finally turning the volume down low.

"I notice you didn't tell anyone else about Ivan's role with Morgana," she said.

"It's need to know."

"And *I* needed to know?" She clutched her chest, mocking Kalene's outburst on our road trip. "It sounds to me like you're divulging Faction secrets again."

"Whatever. At this point, you're like an alternate member. You're on the reserves. Or what do they call it in basketball? You're our sixth man."

"I'd prefer to be the water girl," she said. "Seriously, though—why didn't you tell them?"

"I didn't want to ruin their image of Ivan. Not today."

"Yeah, I get that." She sighed. "We all have our demons, so to speak. Sorry, that was awful. Also, I'm sorry about my dad. I plan to help in whatever way possible. Promise. You know, it's crazy to think, but he could be working with Morgana too. I mean, they're after the same thing, right? The stones."

"I guess. You think he might be?"

She shook her head. "Nah. He's too selfish. That and warlocks don't really understand familiars. Even as a ghost, he'd see her as Jade, an ordinary human."

"But wizards can have familiars, right?"

"I assume. Ivan did."

She dropped me off at my car, which was still in the lot behind Bewitched Books.

"Where ya headed?" she asked.

"Gran's house to visit with Mom. She should be awake. Dave asked me to come by tonight. You?"

"I've actually got another date," Trish said.

"Really?" I smiled for what felt like the first time in ages.

"Yes. Really. Stop grinning like a maniac, or I'll stop telling you about them."

My smile never faltered. "Don't do anything I wouldn't do."

"You know me." Trish's green eyes stopped mid-roll, and she squinted at me as if I'd done something wrong. "Constance," she said, "you shouldn't either."

"I shouldn't what?"

"Do something I wouldn't do."

Trish sped off before she heard my cutting retort. "Huh?"

GRAN'S HOUSE was eerily quiet. I should be used to it by now, but I wasn't. I wanted Gran back. I wanted Brad to get home.

How hard could it be to find a demon who'd gone on sabbatical?

I needed him here. I needed his help.

Brad was the least of my worries. Mom wasn't anywhere

downstairs. She wasn't outside on the porch. When I checked her room, her bed was empty.

I was about to freak out—I was already freaking out—when I noticed the attic ladder was down in the upstairs hallway.

"Mom?" I knew she wouldn't answer. I called her so I didn't scare her. "I'm coming up."

She was sitting at the desk, rocking forward then back. The chair wasn't a rocking chair. The hand mirror was face up beside Gran's other knickknacks. Mom's beautiful reflection dipped in and out of it.

Out of reflex, I went to snatch the mirror away. Mom grabbed my wrist, stopping me.

"What is it?" I asked.

She shook her head.

"Should I call Gran?"

She shook her head again, smiling sadly. She held my wrist in both hands and had me look in the mirror. I saw my blue eyes and my blonde hair. We looked so much alike.

Then it dawned on me.

I smiled too. A tear ran down my cheek. "Yeah, we're related," I said. "You're my mother."

I hugged her as tight as Kalene had hugged me. Maybe tighter.

Before we left the attic, Mom grabbed my hand again. Gently. With her other, she reached for Gran's ruby red ring.

"Oh, no. It's not—"

She slipped it onto my finger.

"It's Gran's," I said. "She probably left it here by accident."

Mom shook her head. She pointed to me.

"Are you saying she left it for me?"

She nodded.

It wouldn't hurt anything to oblige her. It was just a ring. I left it on, and we went downstairs to scrounge up dinner. Thanks to magical shopping, there was chicken and some vegetables in the refrigerator ready to cook.

As I cooked, I talked to Mom like I would anyone else. Even though she wouldn't grasp most of the story, she listened intently. I told her about my day—about Ivan, the demon, Morgana posing as Jade, and everything else.

Just telling it made me exhausted, and I'd had a full night's sleep. Dave was going to be worse off.

"I'll be back later," I said. "I'm going to take some of this to Dave. I'm sure he'll appreciate not having to cook."

Creel Creek was low on fast food options.

After eating and talking to Mom, I was feeling better. Less shaky. I didn't mind driving across town. But it was strange finding Dave's house empty and quiet. The girls were staying over at their aunt's house, which set Dave up for a peaceful night of sleep.

No nightmares.

I left the food in the kitchen and went upstairs to shower. As I got out, I heard the front door open.

Strangely, it didn't close.

"There's a plate in the microwave," I called down. I threw on pajamas and was going to meet him down in the dining room, but his footfalls started up the stairs.

The hairs on my neck stood on end.

"Dave?" I questioned.

A shadow fell on the doorway. It was tall and looming.

"Dave?"

He stumbled across the threshold, and for a moment, I was relieved. It was Dave. He was home, not someone else in his place.

"I know today was hard," I said. "It was hard for me too."

I couldn't blame him for being tired. Still, I thought, he could at least respond.

Dave stayed in the doorway. His face was vacant.

A chill ran down my spine—just like it used to do when I was in danger. I wanted to tell my body off, tell it to stop being stupid. Except it wasn't being stupid. It clued me in.

Dave's eyes were yellow.

"It's you."

"You mean to say it's not your lover." The voice was Dave's, but it had a different cadence, and words were emphasized when they shouldn't be. "He's still in here, you know. I don't take the whole, like the other."

"You mean Morgana?"

"Names mean little to me. Hers, especially so. This isn't the first time she's run afoul of me."

I inched backward, my thigh running into the bed. There was nowhere to go. The demon had me trapped in this room.

I was thankful the girls weren't across the hall. I had other options. If I could spell the window open, I could jump out. And if I was lucky, I might get away without many cuts and just the broken ankle.

Then again, maybe I'd come up with a solution for that problem too.

Trish was right—I was terrible in the moments I needed my powers the most. If only I had a second to think.

"What do you want from me? What's your plan?"

"My plan?" The demon cackled through Dave's mouth. "My plans has *always* been for you."

"Me?"

"Yes. You, Constance Campbell. Daughter of Serena Campbell, granddaughter of Jezebel Young, and descendant of Melvin Creel—the thief who stole my power.

"Who do you think helped Hal Aaron the night he took your familiar? Who else would send the hunter here to slay you? And though countless fools have stumbled upon my magic, pilfering and stealing, it was your family who stole it first."

I'd always assumed Morgana had done all those things. Was I wrong? "Who are you?"

"You already know what I am," the demon said. "Does it really matter what I call myself? What names people of this world use? Names have power, you know. If you keep a name to yourself, you'll never need worry of anyone using it for bad or for good."

"And you can't be summoned," I said, realizing why a demon would protect its name so fiercely.

"True." The sing-song voice went cold. "I made the mistake before. Never again."

"What do you want?" I asked.

"I already told you," it said. "I'm here for you."

I didn't know what it meant, but I did know I wasn't going to lay down for it to hurt me. I had one *other* option. I could fight.

Magic flew into my fingertips. Its energy pulsed in rhythm with my heart, which was hammering so hard in my chest, I was sure the demon could hear it.

"Nah ah." In an unlike Dave move, the demon waggled his finger. "To hurt me, you'd have to hurt him. Is that what you want to do—hurt those you love the most?"

I was mad, caught off-guard, and afraid. The demon wasn't going to tell me its name. It wasn't candid about what it wanted from me either.

Does it want to kill me just because of who I am—because of some people I never met who did things I had nothing to do with?

I couldn't change the past, and from what I could tell, my future wasn't looking too bright.

I jumped across the bed to the space beside the window, my future exit. I held my hands up defensively, not with fists but with my fingertips pointed in the demon's direction.

"Dave's a big boy," I said. "He can take a few blows."

"Is that right?" Dave smiled—or rather the demon smiled with his lips. "If it's so easy to see him hurting, then let's hurt him."

The demon unholstered Dave's gun and pointed it down at his foot.

"No!" I screamed.

"See," the demon said. "Your threats are no longer amusing. I'd hate for this man you love to disappear. Or to hurt those lovely girls of his. I can do both, if you like. Then we can continue our talk."

"What do you really want?" I asked again.

"It's simple. I want you."

I didn't know what I was agreeing to, but I'd agree to anything to save Dave and the girls from harm. "If I agree, then you swear not to hurt them—not to hurt any of my friends?"

"Define hurt."

"Don't touch them," I snapped.

"You have a deal."

"Fine," I said. "Now, tell me who you are."

"Will telling you help you *sleep* at night? If that's the case, then it's best you not know—because I don't want you to sleep, not tonight. Not ever. Listen here. I want you to go to your grandmother's house, stay awake, and in the morning, go out to her porch. There, you'll look up in the sky. And I'll find you then. Do we have a deal?"

"Yes." I wanted to scream. I wanted to cry. I wanted this to be over with.

"Good." The demon glanced out the window. When Dave turned back to me, the yellow in his eyes was gone, as was the demon.

28

IN NIGHTMARES

Dave stumbled and fell face first to the ground.

I checked on him. He was fast asleep. There was no waking him. Even if I could, I wasn't sure I wanted to. Surely, he'd try to talk me out of what I was about to do.

As would Trish. And Gran. Maybe even Brad.

Not like I could blame them. We didn't have the full picture. All I knew was this demon had been out to get me from the start. And it almost had, several times.

I drove to Gran's house with the guilt building up in my stomach. I'd made a deal without knowing if the demon would fulfill its bargain.

Pacts with shadow realm creatures were sealed by magic. But demons are shifty. There were probably a thousand ways it could break its promise.

This time, I didn't tell Mom my dilemma. I sulked beside her on the couch all night and morning. When I felt sleepy, I made coffee. When I got amped up thinking about the demon, I crashed a few minutes later.

My body was no longer built for staying up all night.

Especially after the long day. It took everything I had not to close my eyes for more than a second or two.

When the sun made its appearance, Mom's eyelids were closing. She conked out next to me, her head resting on my shoulder.

I was jealous.

"You didn't say goodnight," I joked. I swept a strand of hair from her face. She looked so peaceful. At rest. "I wish I knew what your dreams were like," I said. "They've got to be better than this."

Gently, I let her head fall to a couch pillow, then I went out through the kitchen to the porch.

There was a chill in the air. Every breath was crisp as a leaf. The sky was a pale blue. The moon was still visible; it hung over the mountains, somewhere between half and full.

I thought if today was my last day on Earth, and this my last view of it, then it wasn't all bad.

"*It's a bird.*" Brad's voice boomed in my head. But the familiar was nowhere to be seen.

It's a plane, I thought, sending the message out to Brad, wherever he was.

"*No. It's really a bird.*" Brad's thoughts were frantic. "*The demon is a bird. It's Vertigo. Ivan's familiar isn't a familiar. Constance, I'm not sure we can trust him.*"

Right.

A lot had happened since Brad left, and really, he'd only been gone a day.

Maybe you want to have a look inside my head at what's been going on since you left? I asked him. I could convey everything with a few simple thoughts and a memory.

What gave me trouble was processing this new information.

"*Oh!*" he said. "*Oh my!*"

It's pretty bad, huh.

"Constance, I don't know what to say except now we know who did this."

Vertigo, I thought. *Yeah, you said.*

"She fits the description of a known demon who was once a powerful ally to many a warlock a few centuries ago. Custos described her as an entity who travels the waking world while her victims are away in their dreams."

That fits with everything else she told me. I conveyed the memory of our encounter with Brad, leaving out the ending. *What happened to her?*

"He didn't know. He said one day she vanished, and she wasn't heard from again until quite recently. But recently to a demon might be different than recently to you."

Right, so, her victims. How did he explain the disappearances?

That's the thing. He couldn't.

The pieces were coming together but nowhere near fast enough. Ivan was killed by this demon—this ally to warlocks.

Why had she posed as his familiar? And why kill him? Why now?

Those were just my questions for Vertigo. She could be here any moment. I looked to the sky, wary of finding her, but it was clear.

Where are you? I asked Brad. I checked around the porch again. No raccoon.

"Still in the shadow realm, I'm afraid. I wanted you to know as soon as I did. It makes sense. I thought it was strange how she communicated with Ivan and never talked with the rest of us. Now we know why."

Why? I asked him. *Why couldn't she talk to you? Aren't you basically the same thing, give or take horns and blackened feathers?*

"It's not quite so simple," Brad said. "There are rules. Just like familiars can't use magic in this realm, demons can't use the shadow realm to speak to other demons. If she spoke to us, she would've spoken through the outside world, and not like this."

It would've given her away.

"Exactly."

Brad, I thought hurriedly, *I made a deal with her—with Vertigo. It's probably a mistake, but I had to. She had control of Dave.*

"It's definitely a mistake," he said. "What kind of deal are we talking about?"

I ignored the question and asked one of my own. *How much longer until you get here?*

"Not long. I'm at the portal now. But Constance, I can't protect you in this world. Not when she's in it too."

That's fine, I thought. *You won't be here fast enough anyway.*

In the distance, a large black bird rode the wind from the foothills. It swooped over the trees behind Gran's house and landed on the porch railing. The raven's cold yellow eyes met mine.

Then the demon, Vertigo, pulled me into her world.

THE OTHER TIME a demon took a ride in my body, I'd been in the backseat attempting to steer. Literally—I was in the car, and Beruth jerked the wheel. My old Subaru flipped into the ditch, and the demon left me there for dead.

I made it out okay, thanks to a psychic's vision and

because the demon was constantly being pulled back to the shadow realm by the spirit of Kalene's mother.

Unlike Beruth, Vertigo walked our world easily. There was nothing, and no one, to stop her now that she had me under her control.

I made a huge mistake, I thought, hoping Brad could still hear me.

There was no response. Not a good sign.

To make matters worse, I couldn't see or hear the real world. I was locked out completely. I stood in a void. A vast nothingness, like an ocean without water, like a dessert without sand.

It was like a dream, and the world a blank canvas.

"What is this place?" I asked aloud.

"This? This is mine." Her words had a musical quality, almost like she was singing a song. "You understand we demons, we each get a world of our own. What you see is supposed to be my realm. It's not much to look at, is it?"

"I suppose not."

"Give it a minute," she cackled.

I felt a tug—a withdrawal—of magic, almost as if I were performing a spell.

The world began to change, painted into a landscape. I realized she was using my magic to do it.

When I tried to use my powers myself, the magic wasn't there. "Is this why you wanted me here? So you could take my magic?"

"It's only fair," she said in her sing-song voice. "As it was your family who stole mine."

I held my tongue but only for a moment. "How did I get here?"

"You fell asleep," she said. "You were so tired, you just didn't know it. We traveled from your dream realm to here."

"So, you use dreams like your own personal shadow realm. A portal to your world. Is that how you disappear people?"

"In a way."

She continued to build out the world with trees, clouds, rolling hills, a stream, and a waterfall. It wasn't original. It was like workplace art—a copy of a copy of a copy.

But the more she built, the more it became real. I could feel the grass beneath my feet and the wind against my face.

"What about the others?" I asked. "What happened to Doug?"

"Doug's life force was infused with magic—magic he absorbed through his interaction with Hal Aaron not so long ago. He built my world for a day. You'll power it for the rest of your lifetime."

I thought about the mine—the rocks infused with magic. Her magic. If there was a way to get out of here, I had to find it. "What about the mine? Why not use it?"

"Your family," Vertigo snapped. "I have no claim on it anymore. I can't touch it. I can't see it."

"But why?" I asked her. "How did my ancestor—how did Melvin Creel steal your magic?"

She painted birds in the sky. A dozen or more ravens. They croaked and called, circling overhead.

"It started, as it always does—with a summoning by a warlock named Samuel Smith. We exchanged magic. We exchanged knowledge. You understand—you've summoned my kind before.

"I was lonely then. I relished our time together. Sam was so smart. So clever. And he saw something in me others had not. Or so I believed.

"He promised me companionship. He promised to show me your world. He promised lots of things. In exchange, I'd grant him power beyond compare—a store of magic to last an eternity."

"Your magic?" I said. "It's what makes up the mine?"

"Now, you're getting it."

"And I'm guessing he broke his word," I said.

"In a way, he fulfilled his end of the bargain." Her singing voice turned bitter. "Sam cast me aside as a pet. A bird. Letting me out to play when it was convenient for him.

"I grew tired of the games he played. Games which he always won. But there was one he lost.

"Sam wad bored and became greedy. The power wasn't enough. He made a deal with a man named Melvin Creel— a swindler who swore they could mine my magic for profit.

"As I'm sure you're aware, it was Melvin's father who founded Creel Creek as a refuge for witches and other magical kind.

"Melvin had his own ideas for what to do with my magic. He wanted control. A fight broke out between the two warlocks, ultimately causing the explosion that doomed the mine and so many of the miners working in it.

"Melvin wasn't a warlock." Really, I had no idea what he was. Just that he was a great great, maybe even another great or two, grandfather of mine.

"What else do you call a man who steals a witch's magic?" She laughed. "Melvin walked away victorious that day, leaving Sam for dead, and casting a spell on the mine making it impossible for me or for Sam to set foot inside it."

"I thought you said he died."

"Sam? Die? Surely, not. I said he was left for dead. You see, Sam's thirst for vengeance is much deeper than mine. He swore to have his revenge on the Creels. And he has. Many times. He killed Melvin. He killed Melvin's son. And his. And the next. Then there was a girl who became a woman, then a witch.

"Sam tried to kill her too, but she proved to be his match. I told you how much he likes games. This game he lost. Badly. He was sent away to the jailer's realm.

"And while he was there, I was freed—free to move about the realms. It was then, when I returned here to my world, I realized my magic had powered this place. My own world had become a prison cell, and I, it's prisoner."

"And now, me," I said. "I guess I should get comfortable, huh."

I wasn't getting comfortable. I was searching for a way out.

I ran through a meadow, skipped across rocks in a creek, and the world kept going and going—drawing from my magic as it continued for what seemed like forever.

There were no doors. No way out. I'd been foolish to think I could stand up to a demon alone.

How long would it take Trish and the others to realize my mistake? And what if Vertigo got away?

What if I'd already disappeared?

I had to buy time.

Still running, I caught up to the void. The land flowed in around me. I ran faster and faster, hoping without hope to find my way out.

"What use is a world if you're not in it?" I screamed.

"You want me there with you? I'm happy to oblige."

A celestial woman manifested in the distance. She was gorgeous, and paler than the space surrounding us. She wore a tattered red dress. Her hair was the same color as her scorched wings. She had mean, yellow eyes, catlike. Her lips were red and full.

Vertigo smiled a devilish smile. "Are you happy now?"

"I just have a few more questions."

I felt small being in the same space—the same universe —as something like her. She wasn't a woman. She was more. And she was the definition of evil.

The demons I'd met before were nothing in comparison to her.

"Listen," I said. "I understand my family hurt you. But it sounds like this Sam guy, he's the real one to blame. There's got to be another way we can work this out."

She laughed coldly. "I'm not interested in more deals with your kind. You'll stay here as long as I want you."

"Okay," I said. "Then you'll keep your end of the bargain —you won't hurt my friends?"

"I won't. No." She looked away, watching as mountains rose on the horizon. Her smile widened. "Others though—I won't speak about them."

"You bitch."

It had seemed so much simpler before—when I thought magic could save the day. And when I thought I could find a way out. I always had before.

"You vulgar witch." She waggled a finger at me, just like when she was inside Dave. "Don't forget, I have the power here. I can inflict pain like you've never felt before."

"Then do it!" I spat.

A fire ignited at my feet, spreading up my legs and chest. The pain was all too real. I screamed in agony.

"Don't ask me to do it again," she said. "I get no pleasure in seeing you suffer."

"But isn't this suffering?" I looked out on her world. "I'm trapped here. I might as well be dead."

She blinked a few times, amused. "Oh, child, you've never seen true suffering."

"True suffering?" I snapped. "Is that what you did to

Ivan? I saw your killing floor. What'd he do to incur your wrath? He had magic. Why kill him? Why didn't he power your world for a while?"

"Is that what you believe?" She smiled again. "You believe I killed Ivan, that I made him suffer. You think I got him in the end for those years he treated me as a pet."

"Wait. What?" I was confused. She spoke of Ivan just as she'd spoken of Sam Smith. "You mean—"

"I mean the sigils on the wall were written in his blood. And he wrote them. It was he who compelled that poor woman with a spell, removing her memories as he so often does, making them seem like a dream.

"He's clever. Cleverer than any mortal I've ever encountered. Or immortal. And much cleverer than you."

"Then why did you lead me to him?"

"It's simple," she said. "It's all part of our new deal. Two birds with one stone. We end the Creel line. And I get my magic."

29

THE RING ON MY FINGER

"Let her go." A voice rang out from somewhere in the vast void of Vertigo's realm.

The world stopped building itself, and the demon spun, searching her world for this new opponent.

I couldn't place the voice, but it was familiar. I'd heard it somewhere before. Sometime before.

Whoever it was, they were nowhere to be seen.

"How did *you* get here?" Vertigo asked.

"It's my daughter you hold captive. Blood of my blood. Kindred in magic. I can find her anywhere she goes. I'd cross oceans, mountains, rivers, and even dreams to ensure her safety."

"Mom?" I sounded like a lost child calling for her mother in a crowded store.

I joined the demon's search. Except unlike Vertigo, whose wary scowl showed fear, I was elated.

I didn't question how she got here. Mostly, I was just happy to hear her voice.

"It's going to be okay," Mom said.

For a moment, I was reassured. I had faith it was going to work out.

Vertigo looked as off balance as I had being thrust into her world.

"You can hide all you want," the demon spat. "It doesn't matter to me. There's nothing you can do here in my world."

"Not true. You don't possess my spirit as you do hers. If you recall, you faced a similar dilemma before."

"And if you recall, you lost that fight."

"True. But the stakes are different now."

Behind us, Vertigo's world began to crumble. The ravens fell out of the sky. The stream dried up. And the lush green grass turned to sand.

"Are they?" A knife appeared in Vertigo's hand. "To me, they look the same."

Pain ripped down my chest.

I looked down and blood was pouring out of a gash down my ribs. Vertigo held the blade ready to swipe again.

I ducked away from her, and she laughed with glee.

"Remember, Serena, if she dies here, she dies there."

"Run," Mom whispered in my ear. "Run and don't look back."

But I couldn't. I was frozen in place. I didn't know if it was my own magic holding me there or if it was just seeing her—seeing her there as a whole woman, a witch in a black dress, and not the shell she was at home.

She smashed a tree down, narrowly missing Vertigo, who swooped away on her broken wings.

She swung around Mom, attempting to swipe me again. Mom was too fast. As they exchanged blows, Mom conjured her own blade.

The realm continued to crumble into nothingness.

I tried to move. I tried to cheer. I could do neither.

Mom spelled a bow and some arrows when Vertigo took to the skies again. She let arrows fly but they turned into blackened feathers before reaching their target.

Vertigo went on the offensive. Lightning crackled across the sky. A number of bolts struck Mom, who took them in stride.

The two of them were evenly matched, my own magic versus my mother's. They both commanded it well. Neither was tiring. But the world was gone.

Vertigo spread her wings and plunged in my direction. She had an angle on me, and I was sure Mom wouldn't get between us in time.

Mom readied another arrow. It flew through the void and into scorched feathers.

Vertigo wailed in pain and frustration. But she got to me first. Her cold hand wrapped around my neck. She held the knife at my side, its point digging into my flesh.

"You really want me to do this?" She spat crimson blood. "I'll kill her. She means nothing to me. She's a host and nothing more."

"You won't," Mom said.

"Why not?"

"I guess you didn't notice the ring she's wearing. Or else you wouldn't have gone near her."

"Ring? What ring?"

"You know what ring," Mom said. "The ring you've been avoiding all these years. The ring my mother wore."

"The ruby." Vertigo's voice was diminished. She no longer sang her words. "But she's gone."

"She didn't take it with her," Mom said.

"But—"

"I know it's hard to lose—especially to someone spell-bound like me. And yet, here we are."

"Her soul is mine. I felt it. I felt the magic."

"You felt what she wanted you to feel. You see, thanks to the ring, my daughter's soul isn't bound to you at all. She was just dreaming and letting your dream rule over her nightmare."

"No."

"Show her, Constance."

I was so confused. But she was right. I could move. I could manipulate the world. I painted the sky blue.

"You can do a lot more than that," Mom said. "You can make a circle and bind her."

I did.

She sulked in defeat, kneeling in the middle of the circle and staring down, to not show us her eyes.

Mom took my hand. "I'll let you choose her fate. You can call Stevie, send her away to prison. Or make a door. Send her to her own world by herself. Lock her in her own prison."

"What if she's summoned?" I asked. "At least with Stevie —in Custos's realm—she can't be summoned."

"True. But remember, there are no life sentences. One day, she'll be free. And her grudge against our family will only be greater."

I wanted to believe it didn't matter. I didn't have kids. But Dave did. And Elsie, if Mother Gaia allowed, was going to be a witch someday. She was going to follow in our footsteps.

I had to make this right. And I had to do it now.

"Here's a door." I spelled a door inside the circle.

Vertigo didn't move or say anything. Her eyes stayed glued to the ground, which was a good thing because a stone appeared at her feet.

"It's not much, I know, but it's what I can spare. If you agree not to set foot in Creel Creek, never touch my friends or family—never see or speak to us again—then you can have it. What say you?"

"I say you're not so clever as your great-great-grandfather, but your offer is fair."

"Then take it," I said. "Leave us and never come back."

30

IN MEMORIES

Mom took my hand, just as I'd taken Kacie's in her dream, and we walked for a while. Ever changing, the dream's landscape twisted like a kaleidoscope behind us. The world wasn't important. Seeing her—hearing her voice—was everything.

"How is this possible?" I asked her.

"Are you asking how I got here or why I'm like this?" She indicated the black dress, but it was hardly what she meant. Mom was together. She was her whole self.

I wanted so much to wake up and find her like this.

"I guess I'm wondering both," I told her.

"We're always ourselves in our dreams," she said. "It's the world we see differently, through the lens of our mind's eye. I've been dreaming about you. Since my return, I've dreamed and I've dreamed about you, hoping you'd invite me in. Tonight, you did."

"Is that how you got here?"

"It is. But there's a more important question to ask. I'm sure you're wondering how we ended up in your dream and not her world."

"I was getting there."

"Brad," she said softly. "Our familiar. He told me in a dream about this ring our family has passed down through generations. He said if I gave it to you, our blood would seal its spell, protecting you from the demon's binding. It's how our family has shielded ourselves from her in the past. But there was always the other threat…"

"Ivan," I said.

"He's gone by many names."

"I don't get it. What did he want? Why was he here?"

"He wants revenge," she said. "He wants to see us suffer. And he believes when the Creels are gone, the mine will return to his control."

"Will it?"

"I don't think so, but let's not find out."

"So, he's not really gone."

"No. The body is, but the soul lives on. He's a shadow hopper—a body thief. He tried to do it to me once, thinking he could get around the spell that way. It almost worked too."

"How?"

"It would be easier to show you."

The world faded to black.

THE DREAM WAS FLOODED with colors and sounds. Finally, it aligned into a clearer picture.

This was more like being possessed by a demon—being trapped inside my own mind. Except this wasn't my mind.

I was seeing the world through my mother's eyes, and the world was a completely different place.

It was an Eighties movie, set in London. Unlike the films

I'd watched from our living room sofa, the world wasn't grainy or faded. It was vibrant and real.

Mom was both the camera and the main character. I could see everything she saw. Hear everything she heard. But I couldn't move around in the same space. See anything she couldn't. There was no going off script.

It was a bright and sun-filled afternoon.

We passed a group of punk rockers, complete with piercings. One had a mohawk a foot higher than the shaved sides of his head.

Mom took long strides, passing shops and people going about their days. Some in suits, some with big hair and bright colors.

She passed several shops before coming upon the Fulham Court Sleep Centre. She opened the door, then the world shifted and Mom was running out of the Sleep Centre and down the road as if something—or someone—was chasing her.

The afternoon had faded into evening, but there were still people on the street.

Mom kept looking behind her. She weaved around shoppers, lost her footing, and collided with a bobby.

He grabbed her by the shoulder before she hit the pavement and pulled her up to her feet. "Is everything all right, miss?"

"Fine," she wheezed, struggling free of his grip.

"You're sure?" He straightened his hat, peering down at her. He had a thick mustache and kind eyes. "Can I assist you in any way?"

Mom shook her head and eased away from him but thought better. "Actually, sir, can you tell me in which direction I can find Madame Tussauds?"

"On holiday then?" This seemed to explain everything.

He combed his fingers through his mustache, then pointed at a street sign. "I'm afraid you took a wrong turn. It's that way. But I doubt you'll make it before closing, even if you run. Next time, try a taxi."

The dream shifted. This time, the hues were muted and dark. Soft yellows and oranges.

Mom was standing in the middle of a ring of wax figures. When she looked at her watch, the world went dark again.

Or I thought it did. Then I saw a lamppost on the horizon.

This wasn't the busy high street. It didn't seem like London at all. More like a village in the country.

Her heels echoed off the cobblestones. Every few seconds, she peered over her shoulder and found no one there.

An owl hooted in the distance.

Every shop was closed up and dark. In front of a tavern, Mom stopped and rapped lightly on the door. "I'm sorry," a man with an English accent said from the other side. "We're closed for the night."

Again, Mom ensured she was alone on the street, before the door opened a crack. An elderly man with a bushy mustache poked his head out. "Did you hear, miss? We're closed."

When he tried to shut the door, Mom put her foot in the way. "Potions and portals," she whispered.

"Mirrors and magic," the man countered.

"You're Oliver?" she asked him.

He nodded then opened the door wide. "Come in. Come in."

The man, Oliver, stuck his head outside. He nodded in satisfaction, closing and locking the door with a bolt.

"You're alone?" he asked.

"No." Mom scooted past him toward the bar. "I came here with another witch."

"Where is she?"

"I, UH, I DON'T KNOW." Mom climbed onto a stool at the bar. She was shaken. She put her face in her hands and sobbed.

"I wasn't expecting anyone tonight," the man said with a note of apprehension.

Her head still in her hands, Mom sighed. "We were supposed to be here tomorrow for our debrief. My partner —Rainbow—she wasn't at the rendezvous point."

"How long did you wait?"

"Too long." The old man went behind the bar. He had trouble lifting the countertop gate. A gray cat leaped up onto the counter. It strolled to the other end of the bar.

"Don't mind her," he said. "My wife's familiar, Morgana."

"You have a wife?" Mom looked around. There were stairs in the back of the bar.

"I used to," he said. "She passed a few years ago. But her familiar's been sticking around keeping an eye on me."

"Oh." Mom didn't know what to think.

Either did I.

"Let me get you a drink," he said. "Any preference?"

"Water is fine."

"Surely, you need something stronger after what you've been through."

"A whiskey then." She lowered her head to the bar. Then I heard words—only they didn't come out of her mouth.

Where are you, Rainbow?

The man put two glasses in front of her and poured from a dusty bottle. "How long have you been with the Faction?"

The whiskey had an odd color, less amber and more brown. I knew that color all too well. It was a potion.

Mom didn't seem to notice.

"Remember," Mom's voice came into my mind, *"I wasn't exactly myself. What happened earlier—my first encounter with Vertigo—it threw me. Now my partner has disappeared. This is supposed to be a safe house. Emphasis on* supposed to be.*"*

So it's not? I asked her

"Keep watching."

I was relieved, at least for the moment, as Mom disregarded the drink. She answered the old man, "About a year. You?"

"Oh, much, much longer." He smiled a toothy smile. "They don't give old Olly here much to do anymore—except tend bar at their meetings. And put up the odd witch or wizard in need. There's a spare room upstairs. I'll make it up for you. Stay here tonight, maybe your partner finds us tomorrow."

"That won't be necessary," Mom said. "I should go. I shouldn't have come here. Actually, she might be at our hotel."

"Could be." He scratched the gray whiskers on his chin. "I don't pretend to know what you or your partner dealt with today. But I know a person in need when I see one."

Who is this guy? I asked.

But I already know, deep down. It was Sam Smith. It was Ivan.

At the corner of the bar, the cat's eyes were locked on the glasses.

"Thank you for your kindness." Mom was about to get up and leave. I could feel her weight shift in the chair.

This movie had turned into a horror film where I knew

the character was doomed but had no clue how the murder would play out.

The man, Oliver, continued to scratch his chin. "I hope, for your sake, that hotel is as warded and guarded as this place is. It might not look like much, but we know looks can be deceiving."

Tell me about it.

Briefly, Mom reached out with her magic. There was a thrum as a magical energy opposed hers.

The old man wasn't lying. Not about that. But we all knew the glass in front of her wasn't whiskey.

Did we even ward the door last night? she wondered.

Her mouth was dry.

"It was a demon," Mom finally looked into Oliver's gray eyes. "What I fought today was a demon."

"What kind of demon?"

"A real nightmare," she said.

"Aren't they all?"

Mom chuckled. "Have you ever fought a demon?"

"Can't say I've had the pleasure. What'd you do to get the honor?"

"I don't really know. This was my first assignment and probably my last. I wasn't expecting them to go like this. I have a daughter at home to worry about. I can't be off fighting demons all the time."

"What about your friend—your partner? Was she fighting a demon too?"

"Different demon. Some idiot's been letting them out."

He nodded. "What happened with yours?"

"She got away. And I guess you're right. She could be anywhere. She could be at the hotel. If Rainbow goes back there, she might be in trouble."

"I'm sure your friend will be fine." He raised his glass.

"Drink! It'll make you feel better. We'll sort this out in the morning."

"I hope so." Mom took the glass. She swirled it without looking down. Then she put her lips to the glass. "Your wife —" Mom stopped herself, "what happened to her?"

"It's a long story for another time," he said.

Mom didn't say anything, but she was uneasy. She tipped the glass. As soon as the liquid touched her lips, she knew she'd been duped.

It didn't matter that she dropped the rest of the drink on the bar. The potion did what potions do. It seethed through her ground teeth. Burned the back of her throat. Stole the air from her lungs. Then drenched her insides with flowing water.

"Are you all right?" Oliver smiled.

Mom tried to fight it. It took a full minute to take effect. But there was no fighting it, not without a counter potion.

She slid off the stool.

Falling.

Falling.

She landed in a heap on the floor, her eyes staring up at the ceiling.

Oliver bent lazily over the bar. "Now," he said, "what to do with you."

He's going to kill me, Mom thought. *He's already killed me.*

But that wasn't true. Not exactly.

Mom's heart had stopped. Her breathing too. But her spirit remained.

There was a jerking sensation like she'd been yanked out of warm bath. Her spirit rose above her mortal vessel— her body—and she stood in the bar as a ghost.

I'd taken the same potion.

I know what this is, I told her. *It's how I visited Dad. He split your soul from your body.*

Mom tried to return. It wouldn't take. "The counterspell is a bit of a doozy," Oliver said. "It requires expert focus and concentration. You've lost your connection to magic. Finding it again is a tough task for a spirit who's never been a spirit before.

"I'll tell you what," Oliver said to her spirit, not her body, which was still on the floor. "I'll guide you to the other side myself. After all, I can't trust you to do it. You couldn't even do me the favor of binding the demon today."

"You sent me here?"

"I am the Faction." The old man laughed. "The Faction is me. And unfortunately, I can't bind that particular demon."

"Your body though, it'll come in handy." He downed his glass.

The old man fell but a blue image remained. In some ways, he reminded me of Gran, of Mom, and of me.

He flew like an arrow, grabbing Mom by the throat. And as he dragged her out through the wall, she looked back. The cat was lapping up the potion she'd spilled.

"This is where it went wrong for him," she said. *"And for me. See, Gran had a feeling she knew who this might be. We set a trap for him."*

The memory continued. Ivan's ghost dragged her through the wall, through the streets, to a cemetery outside of town. In the middle, behind a rusty fence, there was a glowing portal to the shadow realm. He made for it but was yanked to a stop before making it there.

Gran stepped out of the shadows.

"I've waited a long time for this," she said. "Nearly forty years."

"I almost had you then." Ivan's ghost struggled against

his bonds.

Mom, in spirit form, wrenched free. She twisted out of Ivan's hold and joined Gran outside the circle. "You were right," she said. "The Faction is a hoax. It's all him."

"I don't like being right," Gran said. "I love it. It's what I live for. Now, let's settle this score for good."

Ivan panicked as he looked down at a stone circle beneath his ghostly feet. Gran began to chant a summoning —words I knew well.

"No!" he screamed, desperate. "You can't. I'll get you back for this. I swear it."

Custos appeared. He wrapped an arm around Ivan. "Don't forget the terms of our deal," he told Gran.

"I won't," she assured him.

"*But she will,*" Mom's voice said.

Mom returned to the bar, her spirit elated. Even if she hadn't fulfilled the Faction's mission, they'd done what she came here to do. She and Gran had planned this.

And they'd been victorious.

If this is what happened, then why did I go without a mother for my whole life?

"*This is why,*" Mom said.

Her spirit flew headfirst into the bar but stopped short, finding the floor empty. It took Gran nearly ten minutes to make the walk.

"It's gone," Mom told her. "My body—it's gone."

"The familiar," Gran spat. "She did this."

"What do I do?" Mom asked.

Gran looked around the bar to see Oliver's shriveled frame. It was blackened and hollow. No longer a man. "You don't have much time," Gran said. "You didn't take much potion. We have to find a vessel. Fast."

In the distance, an owl hooted.

31

THE WAKE

"Then what happened?" I asked. We were in my dream world again, still walking hand in hand.

A part of me couldn't believe this was real. Another part knew it wasn't, not really. There was a solid chance my memory of this would fade like every other dream.

I couldn't let it happen.

Mom was so radiant. So alive.

I wanted so much for this to be the real world.

The dream shifted around us.

We sat in Gran's living room. Everything was the same as it had been last night.

Mom laughed at the change. "Exactly what you think happened. Gran turned me into an owl. Then she forgot about it."

"But how'd she forget?"

"Guess."

"Morgana." I sighed in my sleep.

I struggled with competing thoughts. While I understood Vertigo's relationship with Ivan or Sam Smith or whoever he was, I couldn't fathom how the warlock and Morgana were connected.

Mom seemed to read my thoughts. "I don't know who she is, except his wife's familiar. I think she came with the magic he stole—whether she was happy about it or not. You saw, she took the first opportunity she had to leave."

"You don't know it was the first opportunity."

"You're right. I don't. But I do know he'd soul hopped before then, so she knew what to expect."

"She took your body for a joyride," I said. "Then she found Brad."

"He made a mistake," Mom defended him. "If I can forgive him, I think you can too."

"I can try." I leaned into the sofa and closed my eyes for a second. When I opened them, the dream had shifted again. We were in the bookstore. The book of secrets sat on the counter.

Mom leafed through it. "My pages are missing," she said.

"I know. I wanted to read them, but I closed it before I had the chance."

"No," she said, frowning. "They're not here. Not even with magic. That's odd."

I let it go because the Faction was a topic we hadn't covered. "What did he mean, he is the Faction?"

"He means he started it. And he ends it. It's a cycle. One of the games he plays. The man's got a savior complex along with several others. He's as twisted as they come."

"I don't get it," I said. "If he wanted to kill us, then why go through all this trouble? We were close to him so many times."

"He can't." Mom snapped the book shut. "There are things in our family history we're never going to know. Magic is complex. So many spells layered upon other spells.

Let's just say, there's a reason we're here in Creel Creek. As long as you call this place home, the man you knew as Ivan can't touch you.

"It's why I brought you here to Gran that summer. We planted the seed just in case our plan failed. Luckily, it didn't. Ivan was locked up with Custos for your whole childhood and up until the moment Morgana brought him back."

"Mom," I said softly. "How do you know all this? How do you remember here but not there?"

She knew what I meant.

"Because here," she said, "I have magic's memory."

"How do we get them back? The *real* ones."

"I wish I knew," she said. Then she squeezed my hand over the counter. "Sweetheart, you need to rest. Really rest. There's no telling what tomorrow brings."

She began to fade.

"Mom," I called. "Can I see you tomorrow night?"

She grinned. "I wouldn't miss it."

I fell into a dreamless sleep. When I woke, I felt more rested than I had in years. And there was a raccoon on my chest.

———

"OH, GOOD," Brad said. "You aren't dead."

"Thanks to you." I rubbed my eyes and looked over to the empty other side of the couch. "And Mom. Where is she?"

"She went upstairs to bed."

"Was she any different?"

"I'm afraid not."

I blew out a sigh and did my best to remember everything that happened in my dreams.

"They'll stick," Brad said. "You used magic. And magic has memory."

"Yeah. Mom said something like that." I stretched and saw the time on Gran's cable box. "Crap! I was supposed to work today."

"You were all supposed to be dead or demonized," Brad said. "I think Trish will understand."

"Maybe. But our customers won't."

I put on my socks and shoes, then ran a comb through my hair. I checked the messages on my phone.

"Anything from Trish?"

"Just a few texts. She's pissed. Go figure."

"Anything else?"

"Some from Dave," I said. "One from Kalene. Ivan's wake is set for tomorrow night."

"Do you think Morgana will show her face?" Brad asked.

"Maybe," I said. "Probably. Unless she's already on the run."

"I'm not sure running is exactly her style."

"Just hiding," I said.

"What better way to hide than in plain sight?"

I nodded in agreement. "Okay. So, what if she's there? What do we do then?"

"I'm still working out a plan," he said. "It won't be as easy as before. She gave up your mother's body willingly because she had a stone of magic to propel her through this world as herself. Unless you're giving them away, I doubt we get Jade's body back in a similar fashion."

My phone chimed with a text.

"Wow!" I blinked and read the text again. "Guess where they're holding the wake."

"I can see in your mind," Brad said. "Unless you'd like to take away my privileges again?"

"No." I shook my head, half in answer and half in disbelief. "Seriously, though, this is stupid. He was killed there."

The raccoon shrugged. "It's not like there are many options. Kalene isn't tight with Cyrus like you are. And would you really want a wake at Orange Blossom's?"

"I wouldn't call us tight," I said. "I'm not exactly on Cyrus's good side right now. The lodge won't even carry his wine. I think I have one bottle left."

"At least *you* can drink alcohol."

I peered down at Brad, and Mom's memories played out in my head.

"What?" Brad hadn't read my thoughts fast enough. It took a moment for him to catch up.

"Oh," he said.

"Oh!" he said again. "I like it. I like it a lot. It still won't be easy."

"It won't be," I agreed. "But maybe, with a little help from my friends, we can work it out."

"Who are you? The Beatles?"

"Sorry. Mom took me to England."

I made calls to Lauren, our potions master, to Trish, Summer, and finally to Kalene, making sure she invited Jade.

We had exactly a day to round out my plan, scrounge up supplies, and pull this off.

⸻

I GOT to the lodge early the following afternoon. As the grocery store manager, Jade was practically in control of Creel Creek's supply of salt. There was no place to get enough to fill an outer circle for Morgana's binding.

Sand would have to substitute. Good thing the lodge had it in spades, to fill its golf course bunkers.

While Lauren and Trish finished the potions we needed, Kalene and I went about sprinkling a thin outer layer around the lodge itself.

The interior courtyard, in its perfect circle, was easier to align but proved more difficult to pull off. For this to work, it had to be salt, copper, or iron.

With a calm, steady hand, I poured the last vestiges of the bar's Margarita salt around the barrier, leaving a single entrance open in hope Morgana would take it without noticing the thin lines around the others.

Kalene tucked a salt shaker in her pocket, so she could close the circle when the familiar arrived.

When we were done, we helped the hotel staff set up the bar, and shortly after, guests began to arrive. It wasn't a large crowd, mostly the Faction, a few patrons of the bar who'd gotten to know Ivan over the last several months, and Jade.

She strode in exactly where we wanted her to. I did a mental fist pump. I slid a pair of sunglasses on and smiled her way. She wore a black dress, something the real Jade would never have worn.

From our time at the grocery, I knew Jade was jeans and T-shirt type. Her formal attire consisted of dark jeans and polo shirts.

"Let's get this thing started," Kalene used the karaoke machine's microphone. Holding up a beer, she made a toast to Ivan.

Others followed. They told stories, leaving out many of the details—like what they were fighting against. Others used the machine to sing some of Ivan's favorite songs.

The whole thing wasn't nearly as somber as I'd imagined it would be.

The five of us, now with Summer Shields, gathered at a table near the bar. "We ready?" Kalene asked. "I'm afraid she's going to leave soon."

"Me too." I nodded. "Let's get to our positions."

Kalene tapped the salt shaker, bulging in her pocket. Summer went to fetch Jade. Trish and I stayed put.

The purpled-haired witch made a face. "Do you think she knows I hate Jade?"

I smiled. "I don't think it matters."

"Case in point, I'm helping out because of the principle. You don't steal people's bodies. That's wrong. Turning them bald?" She shrugged. "That's up for debate."

Summer sidled over with the impostor Jade trailing her. Real Jade would've at least been apprehensive around us. This version beamed with delight.

"Hello, ladies," she said. "It's been a while. I hate we're meeting under these circumstances. As you know, Ivan was a friend of mine. How did you know him?"

"He shopped at the bookstore," Trish said,.

Jade's eyes studied our sunglasses. "I didn't realize it'd be so bright today. I should've brought sunglasses like everyone else."

"Part of a theme," I said. "We're wearing them tonight too. Ivan really loved that Corey Hart song. We'll be singing it later, if you want to join us."

"I'm not sure I know that one," Jade said.

Summer tipped her sunglasses down her nose. "You don't remember *Sunglasses at Night*?"

"Oh, yeah, I guess that does ring a bell." Jade was lost in Summer's eyes. "The music I listen to comes over the grocery intercom. You understand."

"You girls want a drink?" Trish asked.

"Sure." Summer adjusted her sunglasses. She sat down

and patted the next seat for Jade.

"I guess." Jade sat.

Both of them looked at me. "Oh, right. I'll get it. Let's drink something special. Something for Ivan."

"He loved whiskey," Summer said.

"Whiskey it is." I went to the bar. The bartender poured our drinks. I turned my back to the table, so Jade—Morgana —couldn't see what I was doing with them.

I returned to the table and doled out the drinks.

"This is yours." I gave Trish a glass.

Each liquid had a brownish hue, not quite as amber as whiskey normally is. But one stood out. My hand hovered over it. I shook my head and grabbed one for Summer. I put mine down. Then gave Jade the last glass.

Jade eyed the drink warily but didn't say anything.

"Uh oh." Trish pointed over to the stage, and we all turned toward it. "Looks like Lauren's going to do *Sunglasses at Night* without us."

"Can't have that." When my attention returned to the table, I noticed the color of my drink was slightly off.

I picked it up anyway and held it up. "To Ivan," I said.

Trish, then Summer, and finally Jade clinked glasses.

"To Ivan." Jade put her own glass to her lips, but now, she was full-on staring at me, waiting for me to drink.

The potion went down as potions do.

"You thought you had me." Jade laughed. "The sunglasses. The broken circle around the courtyard. Now, this."

"I don't know what you're talking about."

"I switched our glasses. See? This is perfect. I've missed magic. Your body will make an excellent host."

I froze, staring at the brown liquid in my glass.

Gloating, Jade tossed back her own drink. "It stings

when someone's always a step ahead of you, doesn't it?" She took my drink from my hand. "I'm going to need this for what I'm about to do."

"What are you going to do?" I nodded at Kalene.

She stepped outside and salted the exit. Immediately, magic hummed around us, forming a barrier around the bar. It was like an extra gravity pushing in on us.

"No matter." Jade—Morgana—was still confident. "It's only going to make it easier to make sure you don't get away."

Her eyes met my sunglasses. She couldn't hear my thoughts, but she could see the smile on my face. I removed my sunglasses and winked.

"Yeah," I said. "They were all the same potion. The difference with yours was that I put a glamour on it."

"You still consumed it." Her eyes darted around the table. Any second now, our spirits were supposed to detach.

"Oh, I see the problem," Trish said, taking off her sunglasses. "She doesn't know we drank the anti-potion before we got here."

Jade's mouth fell open. "But she—"

"Summer wasn't in on the whole plan. I told her what she needed to know—what you needed to know."

Jade's body slumped onto the table with a thump. A few people looked over. "Too much to drink," Summer said.

The spirit of Morgana lingered in the chair. "So, this is it," she said. "Outwitted by the likes of you."

"Eh, it's more like you were outwitted by an Eighties movie. But I'll take the compliment. I watch a lot of Eighties movies."

Summer gave her a sad smile. "We know you weren't helping him."

"How do you know that?" she asked.

"Let's just say a bird told me. And," she added, "you were just as surprised as I was when he died."

"What was your relationship with him? Trish asked.

"Complicated," she said. "I'll tell you if you let me go."

"No," I said shortly.

With a wave of a hand, Morgana indicated the circle. She glowered at me. "If you know I didn't help him, then what's all this?"

"Uh, you still stole my mother's body and paraded around as her for twenty plus years. Now she's spellbound."

"I had nothing to do with that," Morgana said.

The magical pressure condensed around us as I began a summoning.

"Where—where are you sending me?"

"To a world you're familiar with," Trish said. "Get it?"

She didn't laugh.

Stevie appeared over her chair. In his celestial form, he was as menacing as ever. He gave me a slight bow.

"What do you think? Is a couple of decades enough to set you on the straight and narrow?"

"You're making a mistake." She squirmed as Stevie took hold of her. "I'm the only thing he's ever been afraid of. If you want to beat Ivan, you'll need my help."

"Good thing we'll know exactly where to find you."

With a puff of smoke, the two familiars disappeared into the jailer's realm.

"Do you think anyone else saw that?" Summer asked.

"Not even the smoke," Trish said. "But we've still got to take care of this." She nudged Jade's limp body.

Kalene scuffed away the salt, the circle dissipated, and a cardinal flew to greet Summer by the waterfall.

Compared with everything else, returning Jade to her body was easy.

32

THE OLD OAK

The night wore on. A few more people stopped in at the bar, but mostly, they left. Summer took Jade home. Lauren left with Merritt.

Then it was just the three of us. Kalene threw back a bottle of beer. I shared my wine—the real stuff—with Trish. We drank and were merry.

We barely discussed Morgana or how a modified trick from *The Princess Bride*, my favorite movie, saved the day.

Ivan was nowhere near our conversation. He was an afterthought. Not even a thought. Until, of course, he was.

"What should we do with his stuff?"

Kalene poured the contents of a paper bag out on the table. There was a small black book, several crumpled sheets of paper, and a pair of sunglasses.

"I'll take the sunglasses," Trish said.

I made a face.

"What? I misplace sunglasses all the time. I lost the ones I was wearing today. You can never go wrong with an extra pair. Obviously, we know why he needed them."

"All right." Kalene tossed them to her. "What about this?"

"Is that what I think it is?" I asked.

"It's the register," Kalene said.

I picked up the book and was surprised when I could flip through it. I was even more surprised by what I found inside. Or what I didn't.

"What's wrong?" Kalene asked.

"It's blank."

"Let me see." Trish held out her hand.

"Maybe it was the register," she said. "It's just not anymore."

"No." I shook my head. "It's Ivan. In a memory, he told my mom he was the Faction and the Faction was him."

"So the names inside it are just lost forever?" Trish asked.

"Let me see." Kalene snatched it out of Trish's hand.

"Hey!"

"Sorry. I just have trouble believing it. Now, I want to know if my book's gone blank too."

"Yeah, well, mine's already blank."

"Not true." Kalene shook her head. "If you've read it before, you can read it through magic. You just impart some into the book and the pages reappear. Except these." Kalene creased the book in the middle. "Look at this. These pages were torn out."

"I have a few like that too. I figure they messed up or something."

"Or something," Trish emphasized. "If they messed up, again, they could use magic. Those pages are torn out on purpose."

"Why, though?"

She frowned. "Constance, do you actually know what

happens when you write something in your book? I mean, have you tried?"

"No." I shrugged. "I haven't had much to say."

"What if the secrets have a secret?" Trish asked. "What if you write something down and it makes it so even the people who know the secret can't say what they know?"

"I'd say it sounds plausible. Maybe. What makes you think that?"

She unraveled one of the crumpled papers. It was about the same size of the pages in both the register and the book of secrets. "See this? It's the wrong color paper. It's cream. These are white. This page doesn't belong to this book."

"It belongs to mine." I yanked open my purse and found the book of secrets.

"What does it say?" Kalene asked.

"I can't read it," Trish said, handing it to me.

I read it aloud. "Kalene will forget to chew the gum when she meets the vampires."

"What?" They both asked.

"Stupid secrets." I shook my head. "Never mind. It doesn't matter."

Ivan made it happen. He made her forget. Just like he'd made her forget what she'd stolen from the vampires. I looked at the other pages, but they were trivial in comparison.

"This is how he did it," I said. "This is how he makes people forget."

I went to put the loose papers inside the book, and when I did the book mended. Now, there were only three torn out pages.

Absentmindedly, my finger traced the serrated edges. A flash of purple magic shot out.

"The tree," I said in surprise.

"What about it?" Trish asked.

"Trees make paper, right?"

She nodded. Her eyes were wide as if I'd gone looney. Perhaps I had.

"Magic has memory," I said.

She nodded some more.

"These missing pages—what if it's how he made Mom forget?"

Trish bobbed her head. "I bet you're right. There's still a problem though. You don't have those pages."

"No. I don't."

I thought, and I thought. But nothing came to me. There was no easy solution. I'd already tried to summon those pages once.

I wasn't coming up with anything.

Kalene set her beer on the table. "You said it yourself," she said. "It's a tree. Couldn't you make a few pages?"

"That's not exactly how making paper works," Trish said.

Kalene held up a finger. "Ah, but remember, it's a magic tree."

I smiled.

Kalene had a point. But there was no use getting my hopes up. Our hopes up.

That night, I took Mom out to the graveyard. Like so many times before, we walked up the hill to the old oak tree, and we each pressed our palm to it.

I uttered a spell.

"Tree of unknown age.
Please give us a page.
Help us in our plight.
Old secrets to make right."

A leaf of purple magic grew and grew. When it was about the right size, it fell gently from its branch.

I caught it.

"This is it." I opened the book of secrets. Put the page inside and watched the purple magic bind it with the cover.

Then, in a neat scrawl, I wrote, "Serena Campbell got her memories back."

33

CREEL CREEK AFTER DARK

EPISODE 142

It's getting late.
Very late.
You hear something go bump in the night.
Are you afraid?
You should be!
Welcome to Creel Creek After Dark: Season Two.

Athena: Good evening, paranormal world. This is *Creel Creek After Dark* with your hosts Athena Hunter and Ivana Steak.

Ivana: I'm Ivana and I'd love a good steak. Seriously, I'm hungry for red meat. Is that weird?

Athena: No weirder than usual, Ivana.

Ivana: Also, it feels like forever since our last episode.

Athena: It's been a long time. I agree.

Ivana: And is that a new intro? I like it.

Athena: We've got a lot to catch up on. But first, let's touch on some recent events here in Creel Creek.

Ivana: Did you hear about the storm the other night? I got an anonymous email this morning. Someone says they saw a man standing out in the rain, just past the vineyard. And get this—he was being hit by bolt after bolt of lightning.

Athena: Sounds a little farfetched.

Ivana: No, Athena. It sounds like Creel Creek.

34

EPILOGUE

Figuring I owed him an explanation, I phoned the Vampiric Embassy. The line said it was out of order. Two weeks later, in the wee hours of the morning, he called me back.

"I knew it wasn't a vampire," Carlos said. "Also, I knew I couldn't trust Ivan. He reminded me too much of someone I met in the past."

"It probably was him," I whispered into the receiver.

"Probably," he agreed with a sigh. "You know, I'd say the opposite for you, Miss Campbell. You proved yourself in many ways."

"Were you testing me? Or was it Ivan?"

"Well, you already told me Ivan liked to play games. Perhaps this was one of them. As for me, if I were testing you, I'd say you passed with—what's the phrase—flying colors?"

"I don't know about that. I got lucky. And Ivan got away. I still don't know what he took from you."

"Well, I can tell you. You've earned that much. Ivan took a list of names—every vampire in the United States with their age in centuries, their location, basically everything we have on our kind who've moved over to the new world."

"Wow." I gasped. "Do you know what he's going to do with the information?"

"You might have a better idea than me."

"Not really." I crept out of bed to a sliding glass door with a perfect view of the beach and the waves crashing on the sand.

"Come, now. You've seen what he does. And you know what he wants."

"Power," I said. "Magic. Can you remove a vampire's soul from their body and replace it? Is that even possible."

"Our souls aren't like others. That's not to say it isn't possible."

"If he somehow taps into the magic that makes a vampire a vampire, then he'll be—"

"Powerful," Carlos said. "Immortal. But it's not necessarily a wise move."

"Why do you say that?"

"We vampires aren't without our weaknesses. You've seen firsthand a vampire killed, have you not?"

"I have," I admitted.

"Then be ready, Constance Campbell. When you cross paths with this Ivan fellow again, make him sorry he ever played his game against you."

"I will." I hung up the phone.

"Who was that at this hour?" Dave rolled over in the sheets.

"Just a vampire," I said. "And maybe a new ally."

Trish was right about the ending. Dave was still here with me.

I'd made so many mistakes when it came to love. But Dave wasn't one of them. I fit into his world like a glove.

So what if I'd rushed into our relationship.

I'd rushed into a lot of things—including this world of witches, warlocks and werewolves.

And vampires.

Then again, I thought, *this isn't the end. Not really.*

I'd reached a conclusion—an ending of sorts—and I still wasn't satisfied. It didn't matter if the nightmare was over. Ivan was gone. Morgana was locked away.

Now, it was time to step back—start over and learn who I was as a witch in a world with my mother and without my father.

I vowed to start a new order. Not the Faction but something else—something of my own imagining.

"Come back to bed," Dave said.

Thank you for reading *While You Were Spellbound: Book 6 in the Witching Hour series.*

For more Witching Fun, be sure to check for the next in series: *What Witches Want* or look for other books by Christine Zane Thomas!

ACKNOWLEDGMENTS

Thanks to Ellen Campbell who edited this book. To Paula Lester for proofreading.

Thanks to Jenn for being my amazing partner in this writing journey.

Special thanks to my mother and Don, my sister, and all of my family.

Also to my ClubHouse friends who inspire every day.

ABOUT CHRISTINE ZANE THOMAS

Christine Zane Thomas is the pen name of a husband and wife team. A shared love of mystery and sleuths spurred the creation of their own mysterious writer alter-ego.

While not writing, they can be found in northwest Florida with their two children, their dachshund Queenie, and schnauzer Tinker Bell. When not at home, their love of food takes them all around the South. Sometimes they sprinkle in a trip to Disney World. Food and Wine is their favorite season.

ALSO BY CHRISTINE ZANE THOMAS

Witching Hour starring 40 year old witch Constance Campbell

Book 1: Midlife Curses

Book 2: Never Been Hexed

Book 3: Must Love Charms

Book 4: You've Got Spells

Book 5: As Grimoire as It Gets

Book 6: While You Were Spellbound

Book 7: What Witches Want

Witching Hour: Psychics coming early 2021

Book 1: The Scrying Game

Tessa Randolph Cozy Mysteries written with Paula Lester

Grim and Bear It

The Scythe's Secrets

Reap What She Sows

Foodie File Mysteries starring Allie Treadwell

The Salty Taste of Murder

A Choice Cocktail of Death

A Juicy Morsel of Jealousy

The Bitter Bite of Betrayal

Comics and Coffee Case Files starring Kirby Jackson and Gambit

Printed in Great Britain
by Amazon